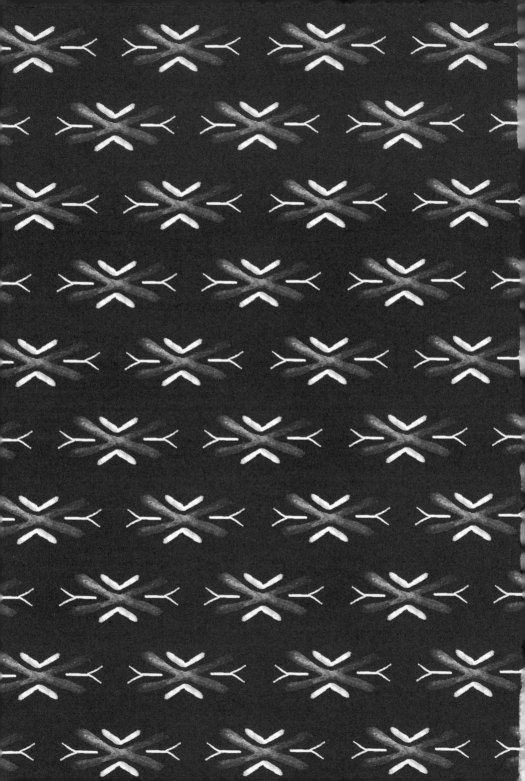

# The LANGUAGE of SPELLS

Library of Congress Cataloging-in-Publication Data:

Names: Weyr, Garret, 1965– author.

Title: The language of spells / by Garret Weyr ; illustrated by Katie Harnett.

Description: San Francisco : Chronicle Books, [2018] | Summary: Grisha the dragon is born in the Black Forest in 1803, the last year any dragon was born, and while young he was trapped by the emperor's sorcerer, and turned into a teapot, which was frustrating but kept him alive while magic and other dragons were disappearing—until one day he meets Maggie, a poet's daughter, and the two of them set out to discover what happened to all the other dragons.

Identifiers: LCCN 2017027778 | ISBN 9781452159584 (alk. paper)

Subjects: LCSH: Dragons—Juvenile fiction. | Magic—Juvenile fiction. | Adventure stories. | Vienna (Austria)—Juvenile fiction. | CYAC: Mystery and detective stories. | Dragons—Fiction. | Magic—Fiction. | Adventure and adventurers—Fiction. | Vienna (Austria)—Fiction. | Austria—Fiction. | LCGFT: Action and adventure fiction. | Detective and mystery fiction.

Classification: LCC PZ7.W5393 Lan 2018 | DDC 813.54 [Fic]—dc23 LC record available at https://lccn.loc.gov/2017027778

Manufactured in China.

Design by Jennifer Tolo Pierce.
Typeset in Warnock Pro.

10 9 8 7 6 5 4 3 2 1

Chronicle Books LLC
680 Second Street
San Francisco, California 94107

Chronicle Books—we see things differently.

Become part of our community at www.chroniclekids.com.

# The LANGUAGE of SPELLS

Garret Weyr

illustrated by Katie Harnett

chronicle books · san francisco

*For Tom Weyr, who
introduced me to dragons*

# The Famous and the Ordinary

**Sometimes, even today, magic still happens.**
Sadly, it no longer comes from cauldrons or fairy god-
mothers with wands. Or even, no matter what you've read
elsewhere, from wizards. Instead, it is tucked into shadows and corners, visible only if you look. But you might
have found it, some years ago, on a cold, rainy night at a
famous hotel bar in the center of an old city in Europe.
Anyone who cared to pay attention that night would have
seen magic coming out of its deep slumber at the exact
moment when an old dragon and a young girl met for the
first time.

The dragon was no ordinary dragon, although Vienna,
the old city with the famous hotel bar, was full of dragons
all claiming to be famous and special. The dragon in question made no such claims. Indeed, he thought of himself

as hopelessly ordinary, especially when compared to his noisy friends at the bar. They never tired of telling their stories about armies, castles, or kings. Our dragon did have a particularly splendid roar, but he'd never used it in battle. Magic had yet to claim him for its purpose, as it had each of his friends. He would have been embarrassed if anyone had told him he was destined for great things. But, in fact, it was why he'd been born.

The girl, as it turned out, was no ordinary girl either, although she would certainly have told you that she was. She believed that mirrors don't lie, and her mirror showed a remarkably unremarkable reflection. The magic that existed in her world sang only in poetry, paintings, colors, or an excellent slice of almond cake. If pressed, she'd explain that her father, a famous poet, and her mother, a dead but still famous painter, were the special ones in her family. She herself, although finally eleven, was just a girl with no particular talents.

Magic is funny in that way: It chooses those who might not choose themselves. In fact, one of the many rules governing the world of magic is that if you pay attention, you will understand how magic has chosen you.

And why.

# CHAPTER ONE

# Forest Creatures

**Back when the world was long ago and far** away, deep in the Black Forest, a new dragon was born. The new dragon was known as Grisha, although his parents, in the strange and mysterious ways of grown-ups everywhere, had named him Benevolentia Gaudium. The grandness of Benevolentia Gaudium, meaning "kindness and joy," was far too grand for daily use, but his parents liked the way it sounded. They had waited fifty years for his arrival, and were naturally thrilled with their son.

Normally it took thirty or so years for a new dragon to arrive in the world, but the special ones took an extra twenty years. No one knew why the world of magic selected particular dragons to be special, but the signs were always clear. One of those signs was the fifty years of waiting. The more obvious signs almost always had to do with an unusual appearance.

So after waiting fifty long years, Grisha's parents were baffled by his ordinary looks. The baby dragon had gold eyes (violet was the most common eye color for dragons, but there was nothing special about gold) and his scales were shades of green, brown, and orange. There was no fuchsia, no blue, nor any red on him anywhere. There was not even the splash of black along the neck that the very best warriors always had. His mother, a National Roaring Champion, and his father, a well-known Sword Warrior and Fire Breather, couldn't understand why they had waited so long for such an ordinary-looking dragon.

But they knew that sometimes magic made an occasional wrong turn. Either their baby dragon was a perfectly normal one, or his particular talent would have nothing to do with his appearance. Grisha's mother shrugged and his father went back to work on the battlefields of men. In a way, it was a relief, for now they would not have to hire one of the older, more experienced dragons to teach Grisha how to manage any extraordinary powers.

Grisha was born in the year 1803, which turned out to be the last year that any dragon, special or otherwise, was born. There is much debate about why dragons stopped being born, and no one knows the exact reason. Perhaps it is simply that in the years following Grisha's birth, the steam engine was invented, railways were constructed, and light bulbs became a fixture in homes and on streets. As the world of men built new and extraordinary things, the world of magic began to decline. No creature lives beyond its own world, and a dragon is nothing if not a creature from the world of magic.

But back in 1803, the year of our dragon's birth, magic was still as common as electricity is today. Dragons, flying horses, and poisonous rabbits roamed Europe's famous forests in large numbers and were not considered, by men or the other woodland creatures, as anything strange or even wondrous. Instead, the dragons, flying horses, and poisonous rabbits were accepted as natural parts of the forest, much like the trees. And if the creatures of magic were obliged to perform various jobs and tasks in the world of men, it just meant that sometimes they were obliged to leave the forest.

Flying horses were used when someone was too ill to send for a doctor or when a message could not be trusted to a servant. Poisonous rabbits, who, save for a small black dot on the back of each ear, looked exactly like ordinary ones, served as both spies and assassins.

Dragons were created solely for battle. Even more than swords, guns, or cannons, dragons helped to sway a military conflict. Almost always, the side with the most talented dragons won the fight.

Fighting was serious business. A good dragon could make or break a royal knight's reputation. Not only that, a single dragon could change the fate of entire kingdoms.

In order to prepare for such a future, you might expect that young dragons would be sent to training camps. Or be forced into childhood battle drills and endurance tests. Or simply take part in endless fighting contests against each other.

But that was not how dragons developed their particular talents. Their parents guided them in certain areas, but before that, new dragons were encouraged to discover their world. As children, all of magic's creatures learned about themselves by being curious about the forest.

It was only when Grisha first crept under a low bush that he learned he could change his size. I'm small, he thought with a mix of alarm and pleasure. What had once been a branch he could trample on was now hovering over his head. When he crawled out he returned to his normal size. To experiment, he sought out a large clearing and, sure enough, he grew in size, able to see over the surrounding trees. Although a bit painful if done too often or too quickly, all dragons are able to scale to size.

In this way, they can easily pursue a fleeing army into a palace or fort.

Grisha learned to fly the first time he'd wandered too far from home and had promised to return before sunset. Without even thinking, his wings spread and he soared into the sky. Over time, he learned how to use scents and an internal guide to stay on route. One trick he learned quickly was, on a return trip, to take off from the place he'd landed. That made it far easier to retrace his route.

Those were the lessons young dragons were expected to figure out on their own. When they were a bit older, their parents taught them how to breathe fire and to develop a unique roar. Tactical lessons in fighting and haunting came still later, after the forest had taught its living things that staying alive mattered above all else.

Grisha loved the forest and all the creatures he met, from the lowly field mouse to the much admired (if rarely seen) mountain lion. He loved the streams, the trees, and the mossy forest floor. Nothing—not a torn paw pad or scraped scale—ever dimmed his spirits. Other dragons were quick to take offense or find fault in the world, but not Grisha. Even when his father died in an unpleasant incident involving a prince and a magic spell, Grisha's sadness was mostly for his mother, whose tears singed her face and gave her a terrible cough.

The older dragon's death happened well before Grisha had had a chance to form any lasting memories of his father. Many dragons born to famous fighters found themselves without one or both parents and without memories of the one who was missing.

Grisha did understand that with his father gone, he would have to teach himself to breathe fire, a task almost always left to fathers. This scared him a bit, as it could be dangerous to learn on your own. The fire dragons breathe is mostly absorbed by their scales, which are designed to help with both flying and fire extinguishing. In the beginning, however, there are always accidents. Grisha singed his lungs, got a very sore throat, and burned the scales all around his nose. Finally, though, he mastered it.

His mother finished grieving rather quickly, for in those days if you were a dragon and your husband went off to battle, the chances were good that he would not come home. She promptly set about teaching her son to roar. Her roar was, without a doubt, the best in the business, and in no time Grisha's roar sounded somewhat like eighteen trumpets, ten bassoons, and a pair of cymbals banging in your ear.

All dragons have roars that sound a lot like military music, but Grisha's had something extra. It wasn't an unusually powerful sound, but every now and again Grisha's roar would make his mother stop, think, and take a good look at the beauty all around her. Perhaps the ability to make others pause would be a valuable tool in battle, she thought. She was curious to see what would happen with her rather odd son.

"Now all that's left is fighting and haunting," his mother said, "but you have a few decades before you need those skills." She had no idea, of course, that those decades and many more would be stolen from him. Her son would never fight or haunt in the traditional sense. However, his roar held hints of what he would accomplish instead—more than she could imagine, which was probably just as well.

Grisha had no sense that either his ear-catching roar or his years-late arrival were the mark of anything special. He was simply relieved that he could put off fighting and haunting.

He usually tried to avoid dragons his age. Their boasting about the armies that they planned to slay and the cities they would one day terrify was fairly tedious. And so, short a father, but in possession of a roar and a somewhat erratic fire-breath, Grisha returned to wandering happily through the forest.

He loved the way the air smelled of cinnamon and rotten oranges. His heart was glad when he heard the forest's streams rushing toward the basin where the Danube River began its journey across Europe. He ate only acorns from oak trees, preferring their dark chocolate taste to the sharp vinegar of a fir tree's cones.

Grisha knew in a vague way that he would one day have to leave. But for now he was content to follow the smells, the sounds, and the feel of the forest. He enjoyed the way his tongue moved to bring air into the part of his mouth designed for smell. Because dragons shoot fire out of their noses, they never use them to smell. For Grisha, breathing through his mouth was an excuse to linger over the first blooms of spring, the wet winter leaves, and the sharp, nutty scent of summer evenings. Grisha would move slowly through sun-drenched clearings, changing size when he pleased and luxuriating in the warm air against his scales.

He'd heard stories about the world of men and how its residents all lived indoors. That life seemed sadly small. Grisha couldn't imagine having to stay the same size to fit into a home's unchanging shape. The silence alone would kill you, he thought. Dragons have such exceptional hearing that they detect even the small sound of a grasshopper hopping.

Most precious of all to Grisha was the ability he had to concentrate even as the most distracting and terrifying sounds were taking place. Men became paralyzed with fear and confusion by battle noises, but a dragon calmly went about the task of fighting. In the forest, dragons were the only creatures who slept through lightning storms, but also the only ones who could hear the first footfalls of an enemy. In this way, dragons bore the responsibility of using their abilities to warn and protect all who shared their home.

# CHAPTER TWO

# The Language
# of Spells

A SOUND ECHOING THROUGHOUT THE FOREST WAS
what lured Grisha from his safe and happy home. It was
very faint at first, but also sharp and clear, as if the rushing
of a stream had stopped to introduce itself. It was a quick,
delicate music that repeated itself over and over again.
The sound reminded Grisha of happiness itself, and he
followed it until he was at the edge of a clearing he'd never
seen before. Through the thick branches of pine trees (the
oaks tended to cluster deeper in the forest), Grisha saw
his first small human. He was so surprised that he almost
breathed out fire. He had to swallow it quickly, which was
very uncomfortable.

Grisha remembered that small humans were called
children and that, as with dragons, there were both boy
and girl kinds. A boy child was causing the sound by shaking a bell, and Grisha was fascinated with its shape and its
music. Near the child there was a quilted blanket spread

across the grass. It was covered with silver and porcelain objects that shone more brightly than water on a sunny day.

If it had been a big human with the bell, Grisha would have turned back into the forest. Everyone knew that the big humans who came to the forest were dangerous. They were in search of unicorns, which was foolish. Any dragon could tell you that unicorns slept all day inside of tree trunks. They only ever came out between midnight and dawn to run, eat, and drink. Occasionally, a unicorn would fall in love with a deer and then would wander with the herd. And, of course, that unicorn would be seen by townspeople or a contingent of knights. Immediately, the whole forest would be swarming with hunters carrying fierce and terrible weapons.

Humans believed that unicorns had magical properties so powerful that their horns could cure illness, stop wars, or help crops to grow. Dragons found this very annoying, since there was nothing magical about a unicorn. The most powerful magic in the forest came from two small rivers that crossed where the great Danube River began. It seemed at once incredible and stupid that anyone could mistake a unicorn for water.

Grisha himself thought unicorns were very pretty, but he knew they caused a lot of trouble. The hunters never found a unicorn and so would become angry. Determined to capture something, they hunted wolves, deer, and most especially dragons. Not just grown-up dragons, but young ones, too.

However, Grisha had never seen a small human hunting in the forest. The sound of the bell was so marvelous that he walked out from behind the pines, not realizing that it would be well over a hundred years before he returned to them. He made his way across the grass and sat down by the blanket, almost hypnotized.

The child, seemingly unaware of any audience, kept shaking the bell until Grisha thought his heart would burst from joy. When the dragon could bear it no longer, he gave a small cough. "Excuse me, small human, but what, may I ask, is that, and how does it make such a wonderful noise?"

The noise, so soothing and gorgeous, stopped. The child whirled around, and in its dark eyes, Grisha saw something that looked like a burning inferno. The air was suddenly heavy and still, as if a storm were brewing. He tried to stand up and run off, but found that he was quite incapable of moving. He was caught in a strong, invisible net. Much to his shock and terror, the small human began to grow, looking like a mud puddle turning into a swamp.

What Grisha did not realize was that the child was not a child, but one of the artisans from Emperor Franz Joseph's private guild of sorcerers, who helped the emperor by making ingenious weapons, poisons, and good-luck talismans.

This particular artisan was famous from Budapest to Vienna. His name was Leopold Lashkovic, and he was the emperor's chief sorcerer. With a great deal of practice and hard work, Leopold's powers had increased from transforming people into animals to changing his own shape whenever he liked. But his real talent was making objects so beautiful that people paid vast sums in order to possess them. In this way, Leopold's talent earned money for the emperor, who desperately needed it to pay for his castles, his soldiers, and his collection of crowns. His service for the emperor was only one of the reasons that Leopold was known as the most powerful sorcerer of all time.

Leopold loved money more than anything else in the world. His love of it increased his powers because magic demands that the people who practice it give up something precious: time, money, or something they love. And once that precious thing is given up, it can never be returned, no matter what.

Haven't you ever wondered why, in a world where magic still lingers, you are unable to use it? The reason is simply that only a very few people can give up something they love. And of those very few who *can* give up something precious, most choose not to.

Leopold Lashkovic both could and did.

The fact that what he loved was money made him far more powerful than a practitioner who simply gave up time or a beloved item. Because Leopold was giving up two things on magic's list of demands—money *and* a beloved item—he was very, very talented.

Leopold's objects—tiny teapots, huge vases, ornate hand mirrors, and ruby rings—were made mostly with the usual things: bronze, silver, gold, precious gems, and pearls brought up from the bottom of the sea. But he would mix one secret ingredient with these ordinary elements to produce an object that could be sold for as much money as the emperor needed.

The secret ingredient was almost always a creature whom Leopold lured from the forest with one of his magic bells. Usually it was a young creature, for they were still full of curiosity and willing to follow a beautiful sound.

Like most members of the emperor's guild, Leopold was anxious to capture a unicorn. You would think that such an advanced practitioner of magic would know that a unicorn was worthless, but living in the world of men can make even the wisest sorcerer believe in foolishness. Therefore, Leopold had been working on his bells for years, trying to find the right sound to lure a unicorn. He had bells for rabbits, wolves, deer, foxes, and even chipmunks. He'd caught a flying horse more than once, but the bell Grisha had followed had been Leopold's latest effort at unicorn hunting.

"Not bad, not bad," Leopold said, when he was done changing shape from child to man. "A dragon's almost as good."

And then Leopold began to rummage through his pockets, speaking in a language that Grisha had never heard. This was extremely frightening, because Grisha, like all dragons, had been born knowing German, English, Japanese, Chinese, Norwegian, Hungarian, Serbo-Croatian, Czech, Ukrainian, and a smattering of French. He had a terrible feeling that Leopold was talking in the language of spells.

Leopold pulled a glass vial from a pocket near his left ankle and began walking around Grisha. As he walked, he waved his hands, and a great cloud of grit, dust, and sand rose and flew over, under, and through Grisha's scales. It moved into all of the soft bits a dragon tries to protect: nose, eyes, and paw pads.

Unable to sneeze, but desperately needing to, Grisha felt his scales tighten. And then, all at once but also slowly, he felt himself melting, bubbling, dissolving, and turning into a cool, elegant surface. Grisha could still see, hear, and think, but he was no longer the young dragon who joyfully walked through the forest. He was a teapot.

At first, all our dragon could do was panic, which is hard when you can't move or breathe. And since Grisha couldn't swing his tail from side to side or scream for help, he was reduced to pointless thoughts racing around his mind.

He was unable to take a calming breath, and each time he remembered that he couldn't breathe, his thoughts would scream out: I can't breathe. Oh, no, no, no. Finally, exhaustion settled Grisha's mind. The chill that comes when you are enchanted into an object focused his panic into one thought: I'm so cold. I'm so horribly cold.

It was a painful and chilly journey from forest life, so full of sun, foods, and sounds, to a small teapot that offered only the limited comfort of gold and rubies.

But Leopold Lashkovic hadn't simply turned Grisha into reds and golds. His entire shape had become that of a small teapot. His long neck and head were a spout, and his tail was a handle. His body swelled out to allow for hot water and tea leaves. His wonderful wings were curled up into a lid, and his once magnificent feet were now simply part of the teapot's base. His eyes were still gold, but no longer a dragon-shade of gold. They glowed as all precious metals do, not as eyes full of sight.

Leopold Lashkovic picked up the pot and studied his handiwork.

"Perfect," he declared. "This will fetch a nice sum."

# CHAPTER THREE

# Dragon in a Teapot

**Leopold carried Grisha to the royal court of** the emperor, who was so taken with the teapot that he refused to sell it, keeping it for himself. Leopold was very annoyed, since the whole point of his creations was that they be sold to make money, and he wondered what it was about this ordinary-looking dragon that had caught the emperor's fancy.

Leopold studied the teapot and tried to determine whether Grisha had some sort of hidden power. But in spite of his cleverness, Leopold could not identify what made the captured dragon special.

Franz Joseph, the emperor, never wondered if the teapot had a hidden power. Instead, he was content to have the gold-and-ruby dragon in his jacket pocket or nearby whatever room of the palace he happened to be in.

Grisha tried to take an interest in his new and perplexing surroundings, but for the first ten years or so, he was too sad to pay attention. He had been barely fifty or sixty when Leopold Lashkovic captured him, and he spent the next decade thinking his life couldn't possibly get any worse.

Life in the teapot was a cold, unmoving, isolated one. It was so unbearable that he often wished the emperor would drop him. If the teapot would shatter, then maybe his terrible existence would end.

So, it's come to this, Grisha thought. You want to die. Buried deep inside his gold-and-ruby self, Grisha thought he heard a rebellious NO! But it was hard to tell. In spite of once having exceptional hearing, Grisha was now incapable of hearing even himself.

Often, after slipping Grisha into his pocket, Franz Joseph would go to the palace's great hall, where all of his ministers were waiting with folders full of complaints and problems.

The emperor had to sit still for a very long time, which meant that Grisha was stuck inside a jacket pocket. It's the worst kind of dark, he thought. In the forest, the dark promised evening's sounds and breezes. The dark inside of a jacket pocket promised nothing.

Finally, Franz Joseph would return to his rooms and order his meal. One evening, he also asked for a fire to be lit. He put Grisha on a small table next to his favorite chair, threw his jacket on the floor, and sat down. Normally, the emperor preferred sleeping and working in a cold room, so this was the first time Grisha had seen a fire since his captivity. It was also the very first time in his life he'd seen a fire begun on purpose that wasn't part of a dragon's breath. He was too far back from the flames to feel any of the fire's heat, but the familiar sight of orangey gold leaping into the air was wonderful.

Grisha noticed that around the wood, the fire was quite blue. He tried to remember if that had been the case in the forest, but a forest fire was always an accident and something everyone rushed to stomp out. No one ever stopped to study its colors.

The hot meal arrived, and Grisha looked closely at the strange things humans ate. He had been present when Franz Joseph ate dinner before and had also gone to banquets in the emperor's pocket, so he knew what humans called food. But other than noticing that they didn't eat acorns, he hadn't paid any attention. That night, however, the dinner tray was placed right next to the small dragon teapot.

He looked at the lumps of light brown meat nestled on a bed of wide yellow noodles. Humans called it goulash. A gold and crystal glass held a dark red liquid that was wine. On the emperor's tray was a plate of soggy-looking lettuce that no self-respecting rabbit, poisonous or not, would touch. No one in the palace ate much that resembled what a dragon might like to eat, Grisha observed.

Eating was one of the many things Grisha missed, and he wished that he'd appreciated his meals more. Franz Joseph ate only a little and hardly touched his wineglass. He didn't appear to have enjoyed much about his meal, and in trying to imagine why, Grisha saw that the emperor had deep lines by his eyes. When the emperor wasn't chewing, his mouth was pulled into a tight, thin line. From time to time, he rubbed his temples as if his head ached.

He's unhappy, Grisha thought, astonished. After all, the emperor was a free man. He was able to walk outside, stand in the sun, sit near a fire's warmth, and eat anything he liked. Why would he be unhappy?

Just then, Grisha realized something incredible. He wasn't cold! Not even a little bit. The forest had taught him to explore his world with curiosity and now Grisha understood why. When watching the world, he forgot his own troubles. Simply taking an interest in the world meant that he stopped wishing to shatter into pieces. He was still lonely, often sad, and usually freezing, but now, at least, he wanted to live.

During the next almost five decades that Grisha spent with Franz Joseph, the dragon never figured out why the emperor was unhappy. However, Grisha watched his owner carefully, and when he was in a dark pocket, he listened to what he could. Some of the talk was interesting (laws, weapons, and visitors from distant lands) and some was not (taxes, crops, and sanitation). Grisha kept hoping that he would hear about another dragon, but he never did.

And then one summer, some fifty years after Grisha's capture, it seemed that all anyone spoke of was a fierce and bloody war that had broken out across Europe. The archduke of one country was shot and killed in another country, making every king, emperor, and minister angry enough to send huge armies into battle. If that sounded like a silly reason for a war, well . . . there were other reasons, but hardly anyone remembers them.

Grisha could tell by the emperor's constantly trembling hands and the hushed voices around the castle that everyone was deeply afraid. He wished he could offer advice. Find a dragon, he wanted to say. The more talented your dragon, the better your chances of winning are. He had no way of knowing, of course, that guns and cannons had replaced both swords and battle-ready creatures of magic.

Grisha tried mightily to understand the different things he heard. Franz Joseph received weekly updates about invasions, military ministers, commanders, and bombardments. With no idea of what a bomb was, Grisha wondered whether "bombardment" was an emperor's word for magic.

At night, when the palace was quiet, he would think about the dragons his age whom he had avoided because of their tedious boastings. Battles were places where metal swords and spears crashed against one another, horses reared up, and dragons roared out fire as they trampled soldiers underfoot. While free in the forest, Grisha hadn't wanted to think of such things. Now, far from home, Grisha fervently wanted the chance to fight. I've heard enough, he thought. He wanted to live his own story instead of only listening to others'.

And then, before Grisha could discover if any dragons were fighting in Europe, the emperor fell ill and died.

Grisha realized that he had spent more time with the emperor than he had with his own family. I have more memories of Franz Joseph than of my father, Grisha thought, so shouldn't I miss him? But he didn't, as it is next to impossible to miss someone who never spoke a word to you.

As Grisha was trying to sort out his feelings, he was unceremoniously wrapped up in old newspaper and tucked into a box. All of the emperor's possessions were packed up, to be sold or given away. Grisha looked around his box. Careful observation revealed that he shared the small, dark space with cuff links, diamond-edged picture frames, and a set of gold-and-silver coffee cups. He imagined nodding hello to each of them. But, of course, he couldn't move, and nothing in the box greeted him.

Grisha was soon collecting dust in the window of a shop, which was a new kind of prison. The coffee cups had been bought right away, as had the cuff links and picture frames. Grisha resigned himself to an eternity of watching the same street, but also felt his natural cheerfulness slowly returning. For one thing, the sun regularly found its way onto the spot where he stood, which meant he no longer had to work to forget how cold he was. Instead, during those periods when the sun glinted off his gold-and-ruby exterior, he was warm and toasty.

The street, while never changing, did offer the sight of people coming and going. Grisha tried his best to observe them, but they moved so quickly it made him dizzy. So now he had some warmth, but also a queasy feeling to go along with the lonely ones. And even though he'd never been terribly talkative while in the forest, he found himself desperate for someone to talk to him.

I don't even have to talk back, Grisha thought, which was just as well, since he couldn't say a word.

Finally, on a warm summer day, Grisha's life took a turn for the better when a man happened to pass by the shop. Something clearly caught the man's eye and, for several moments, Grisha had the feeling that the man was looking right at him: his true dragon self, not the teapot jail. Then the man took out a pocket watch. Grisha held his breath, hoping the man wasn't late for something that would take him away. The man looked from the watch to Grisha several times before he snapped it shut and entered the shop.

The clerks and even the shop owner made quite a fuss over the gentleman, ordering up a tray of savory sandwiches and some strong tea with sugar and milk, which were scarce during the war, so right away, Grisha knew that this was no ordinary customer. And just when he'd decided the man was clearly too important to care about a dragon-shaped teapot, Grisha was retrieved from the window and placed in the man's hands. It felt as if they were studying each other carefully.

>—•—<

Yakov Merdinger, for this was the man's name, wasn't simply a charming, clever man who worked at his uncle's bank. It was a widely known fact that Yakov had money—which, as the war dragged on, fewer and fewer people did—and that he used it to help others. He was famous throughout Budapest and beyond for knowing How To Get Things Done.

It was well known that the banker's clever nephew could find food, railway tickets, heating fuel, and even butter, despite all of those things being very hard to get. Once Yakov had those items, he knew how to give them to those in need. And he did it without ever making anyone feel that they were receiving charity or pity. He had, people said, a magic touch. That wasn't true, but he liked that it was said.

As a very young man, Yakov had wanted to be a magician. He was interested in learning how magic could help others. For a few years, he had even traveled with a circus and studied with some of the best scientists and magicians in Europe. In the end, though, he realized he was limited.

Magic, you may remember, demands that the people practicing it give up something precious: time, money, or something they love. You can never take back what is given up, either. Yakov simply wasn't willing to give magic all that it required. He wanted to do other things in life as well—work for his uncle, enjoy life in Budapest, and help the poor.

So he gave up his dream of becoming a magician without ever forgetting it. The only thing he allowed himself to save from the world of magic was a potion he'd purchased early in his studies that allowed its user to see magic in a world where it had mostly vanished. He put a few drops of the potion into his coffee every morning, hoping to catch a glimpse of the magic he so loved.

And so, unlike anyone else, Yakov was able to see through Leopold Lashkovic's spell.

While he didn't know the particulars of the dragon in the teapot, he knew that there was a living and breathing creature in there. That was why he had stopped what he was doing, gone right into the store, and paid a nice price for a small teapot. He took it home to remind him of his old passion.

Which is how Grisha, at long last, made a friend.

# CHAPTER FOUR

# LIFE WITH YAKOV

**IN HIS NEW HOME, GRISHA SAT ON A DESK, WHICH** he was very grateful to find was right by a window. Yakov was careful to always place a hot bowl of soup or cup of coffee by the gold-and-ruby dragon. As he did so, he would often say, "I suspect it's cold in there, my friend."

Grisha appreciated the warmth and wished he could thank the cheerful, kind man. It was so good to be around someone who knew he was alive—and even though Yakov was clearly busy, he never forgot small courtesies.

Grisha had quite a bit of time to study his new companion, and had come to the conclusion that Yakov was perhaps not what humans called handsome. Yakov was short, and his features were not precise or imposing like the emperor's. But Yakov smiled a lot and his eyes gleamed in a way that let you know he was happy.

Yakov liked to listen to the news on the wireless, but he also loved music, and Grisha began to appreciate how a violin, a cello, or a piano could be as lovely as a running stream or the sound of horses playing. After he and Yakov listened to music, they would both sit in silence for a while before Yakov announced he was going to bed.

"Sleep well," he would say to Grisha. "May we meet in the morning."

>—•—<

The banker and the dragon had barely settled into a routine when the war ended. All over Budapest, there was a sigh of relief. People no longer called it just plain "the war," but instead used "the Great War" because it had been so big and bloody. There was almost no time to get used to the peace, for Yakov's uncle decided to send him out of the country. Yakov's new job would be running the bank's English branch.

"We're off to London," Yakov told Grisha, who thought, I hope it will be warmer there.

Yakov packed a small suitcase of clothes and two trunks full of books. He put the carefully wrapped teapot in a leather case that held all of the bank's important papers. Grisha traveled in style, tucked inside a silk-and-cashmere blanket.

The English sky was gray and the air was almost always damp. People drank endless cups of tea in an effort to warm themselves, but it never really worked. Not unless you drank it wrapped in woolens while sitting directly in front of a fire. Since almost no sun came through the windows, Yakov put Grisha as close to the fire as possible.

During the day when the rooms grew cold, Grisha kept his spirits up by looking forward to Yakov's return. Not only would Yakov light a fire and put a warm drink next to the dragon, he was also bursting with stories about his new life, which was both hard and exciting.

Yakov spoke excellent English, but with an accent. Although his clients at the bank thought he was a fine fellow, he told Grisha how it was hard to make friends in a city that did not, for the most part, like foreigners. People did invite him out, as happens to men with money and no wife, but Yakov often felt alone and as if he were the only Hungarian in London.

At night, before bed, Yakov wrote letters to his parents, who had stayed in Budapest; to his uncle in Zurich, where the main branch of the bank was; and to his cousin Itzhak, who had gone far, far away to America. Grisha loved to hear the letters, which Yakov read aloud, checking for any mistakes, before slipping them into their envelopes. Yakov wrote about London and how the city was at once beautiful and horrible, full of lavish dinner parties as well as cold homes in which no one had enough to eat.

Yakov wrote once a month to his father, twice to his mother, and twice to his uncle. But it was the weekly letters to Itzhak from which Grisha learned the most. Those letters were full of news, theater, art, and politics, and also how terribly hard it was to go through life with no one to love.

London was bustling like never before as everyone rushed to forget the Great War and its bad times. Grisha could feel the energy, longing, and excitement of the city's residents. It pained him to be in his teapot prison, but in Yakov's letters to Itzhak, he had the chance to hear all about those who were free.

Grisha looked forward to these letters in the way he used to look forward to an oak tree's acorns. He knew Yakov was lonely, and he liked to think that he and Itzhak kept him company as much as a teapot and a cousin in America could.

Grisha, of course, was also lonely, but by now he had been a teapot for longer than he had been a dragon. He was more used to his loneliness than Yakov was to his. He still missed the forest, and he longed to do more than sit and listen. His desire to take part in life, and to have an adventure of his own, grew with each passing year.

For now, though, he loved those moments when Yakov looked at or spoke to him. It was then that Grisha felt alive and free.

Those moments would pass, of course, and he would remember that he was not alive, but buried alive in gold, ruby, and porcelain. Nonetheless, being with Yakov was, so far, the best part of being a teapot. The apartment in London was a far less bleak place than the emperor's palace.

His new owner's loneliness did not last forever, thankfully. It was in a letter to Itzhak that Grisha first heard important details about a young woman whom Yakov had met at a party. She spoke English with a Hungarian accent, in spite of having lived in Paris for a long time.

Her name was Esther, and she taught at the Royal College of Music. Grisha listened to this particular letter with special interest—he clearly remembered Yakov's joyous face the night he'd returned from the party.

*She has studied with Nadia Boulanger and lives with her father in a small apartment that smells a lot like the homes of our childhood. Her father was an accomplished violinist, but his hands are now old and stiff. Sometimes I take her to the moving pictures. Have you been to one of those yet, Itzhak? They are quite marvelous. Please send me stories from your new life.*

*The family and I are so proud of you.*

*So much love, from your cousin Yakov.*

Yakov and Grisha ended London evenings the same way they had in Budapest. After the news, music, or letter writing, Yakov would take his leave, saying, "Sleep well, may we meet in the morning."

And in the morning, after his breakfast and shave, Yakov would take his potion out of the same cabinet that held his writing supplies. He would pour a little into his coffee and look at Grisha while he drank it. "My friend," Yakov would say, "I don't know what misfortune turned you into a teapot, but I wish you well."

Grisha would have done almost anything for the chance to explain about Leopold Lashkovic and the magic spell, but he took solace in knowing that, even without hearing the details, Yakov was sorry about what had happened. For his part, Grisha wished that Yakov would live forever, as he had no desire to ever again be stored in a warehouse, sold in a shop, or live in a different house.

Especially not when this one was so interesting. From his spot near the fireplace in the front room, Grisha got to hear when Yakov asked Esther's father for permission to marry her, and he was there at the big party to celebrate Yakov and Esther's wedding.

Esther was small and round, happy and cheerful. She filled the large, empty flat with laughter, love, and more music than ever before. She played the piano for hours during the day, practicing or giving lessons. Her piano was in a different room from Grisha, but its sound soared into every corner of the apartment.

If the years had dragged for Grisha with the unhappy emperor, living with Esther and Yakov, who took joy in their lives, made time move far more quickly.

Soon two small children ran through the rooms, their sticky hands grabbing what they could and their little legs tumbling over everything. Their names were Rachel and Ella, and they each had a mix of Yakov's thoughtful curiosity and Esther's cheerful manner. Grisha loved watching them as they grew from small infants into one mischievous girl (Rachel) and one serious one (Ella).

Rachel and Ella adored Grisha and often asked for permission to take the teapot into their room at night. "He will protect us while we sleep," Rachel announced.

Having spent many an hour staring at her father's gold-and-ruby-encrusted dragon, she had concluded that beneath the jewels lay a living, breathing creature. Some people simply know things without understanding or caring how they know, and, as a child, Rachel was one of those people. She easily saw what her father needed a potion to see.

"We like him," Ella added, not convinced that the teapot dragon was real, but still anxious to have it in the room at night, as there was no mistaking that she slept better when it kept watch.

So every night, after the family had eaten and then started up for bed, Grisha would make the journey to the children's room. And every morning he would be brought back down to the front room. Of all the things Grisha observed from within the teapot, the most thrilling was watching the girls grow from crawling babies to running children, into what Esther called girlhood.

Although Ella remained uncertain about the actual life inside the small dragon teapot, the curiosity in her eyes when she looked at him was enough to make Grisha feel recognized. She never spoke to him, but Ella's gaze told him how much he mattered to her.

"Hello, dear one," Rachel, who spoke to him often, would whisper in the mornings, as if they shared a secret.

And from time to time, she did confess to Grisha all the small misdeeds of her day. They were never more serious than hair pulling, rude thoughts, or messy drawers. The small, trapped dragon grew to view Rachel's hushed admissions as something as precious as warmth.

Before the girls were born, the only child Grisha had ever seen had been Leopold Lashkovic in his little-boy form. The dragon had no idea how the girls would turn into fully grown humans, but he hoped that no matter how it happened, they would remain happy, healthy creatures.

Each day, after breakfast and music class, the girls had their main lessons from a governess, who then turned them over to a maid for walks in the park. Whenever Rachel and Ella came inside from playtime, he was reminded of fresh air, of sun and birds, and of all the things he missed by being in a teapot.

Sometimes life wasn't what you wanted, but it was still life. And Grisha, a creature of the forest, knew that being alive was what mattered most. He told himself he was happy, and it wasn't wholly untrue. But neither was it wholly true.

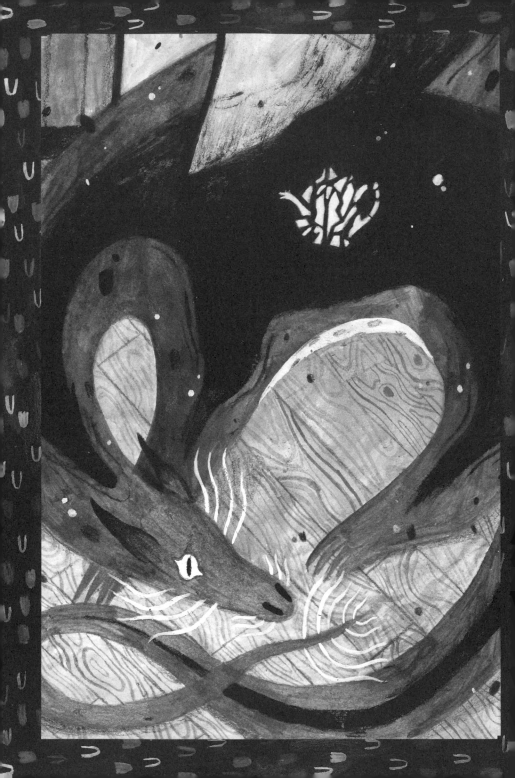

# CHAPTER FIVE

# WET LEAVES
# AND CANDY

**IN THE EVENINGS, ESTHER AND YAKOV SAT IN THE**
front room talking about the girls, work, and the news.
They didn't simply read the paper or listen to the wireless, but discussed in great detail what was happening in
the world. Grisha, who so longed to be part of the world,
listened with sharp attention. Hard times were everywhere again, and people were losing their freedom along
with their jobs and their money.

One country took over another country, and the
letters Yakov wrote to Itzhak now carried almost nothing but bad news. A new war was coming, and this one
would be the Second World War, it seemed. The Great
War would now be called the First World War.

I am thoroughly sick of wars, Grisha thought, no
matter their names. From listening to Yakov and Esther,

he knew that this war would have stronger bombs along with the same bloody battles as the last one.

Yakov, too, was sick of wars and worried about how hard they were for ordinary people. He sent money and tickets to his parents, urging them to leave Budapest and come to London. From London, Yakov had decided he would send them, along with Esther and the girls, into the countryside. He had already found a home in a small village, far away from any cities. The family would be safe there, Yakov said. His uncle would wait out the war in Zurich, and Yakov would remain in London to take care of the bank.

Grisha fiercely missed the girls and Esther, but when bombs began to fall over London, he was happy they were gone. Londoners, who were being bombed every three or four nights, called it the Blitz. Sirens, explosions, dust, and terror hung over the city like snow clouds.

Yakov was able to find tea, butter, bread, and medicines, all of which were in short supply. He sent them not just to his family, but to almost every family he knew. Alarmed by this behavior, his uncle wrote stern letters from Zurich, lecturing on moderation and on not allowing Yakov's generosity to spend the family into the poorhouse.

In a letter to Itzhak, Yakov explained his actions.

*I can think of no more satisfying way to lose the family's money. My children, wife, and parents are alive and safe. How dare we not help those in need?*

As a creature of the forest, where helping any creature in need was the law, Grisha supported Yakov's thinking. At night, when Yakov sat with Grisha, he read the paper or listened to the radio. When the air-raid sirens rang out, he switched off the lights and drew the blackout curtains. There were shelters, but Yakov disliked them, preferring to take his chances by remaining at home.

When the Blitz ended, Esther returned to London, but the girls and their grandparents remained in the countryside. Things were safer in the city than they had been, but the war was farther away if you were in a small village. Esther worked at the military hospitals, helping the wounded and the shell-shocked. She gave concerts for grief-stricken families and, with the nursing staffs, kept the supply closets clean, stocked, and organized. Yakov kept giving away supplies. Grisha, as always, kept watch.

>•<

Slowly the tide began to shift. The heavy clouds of war gave way to rumors of peace. Children returned to

London, among them Rachel and Ella. Grisha thought he would burst with joy when he saw the girls again, taller and more like young women, but still his beloved girls.

Other changes were small, but Grisha, in the habit of observing them, saw every difference. Rachel was more serious about her studies than she had been, while Ella spent more time at the piano. It seemed to him that war had made everyone a bit more serious. But it was clear that joy and laughter were part of the family's lives once again.

The war, which had dragged on for six years, was finally over. Like all good news, it came with bad. As part of the peace, Europe was cut in half, with the western half going to one of the war's two winners and the eastern half going to the other. Everyone in every country, east and west, was exhausted and anxious for good news.

Grisha wondered what had happened to the creatures of the forests. It didn't sound as if magic had had any role in deciding how to divide the world.

News about his fellow dragons finally did arrive, but not from Germany. Instead it came from Vienna, where Grisha had lived with the emperor. Yakov's uncle wrote from a place called the Hotel Sacher—Grisha noticed that on the stationery—where he was staying during a long trip, on banking business.

The soldiers who are in charge here suddenly have a problem that is literally bigger than all of the others: dragons. No one knows why or how they came to Vienna, or what on earth to do with them now that they are here all of a sudden.

No one has seen so many dragons in one place in more than eight years. I thought they were residing permanently in Europe's forests. Almost all of the creatures claim to have followed a sound, but of course no one believes them. What sound behaves like a map to Vienna?

The soldiers have paid a huge sum to a man who has experience with such problems. He promises that any dragon not in Vienna for registration will be sent in a sealed train to Siberia, beyond the Ural Mountains. Meanwhile, the soldiers have put up the dragons in all of Vienna's fine hotels. I see them milling around the Sacher's lobby, waiting to be registered and assigned jobs.

Siberia is a terrible fate for anyone, and these giant creatures seem harmless to me. They are sad and lost-looking, just like every other refugee you see these days.

*The soldiers clearly hope the man they've paid
will know how to handle this particular problem,
so I expect they'll sort it out. Now, if they can
just get Europe itself restored, all will be well.*

*Love to you and Esther, yours, etc., Uncle.*

Yakov read this letter three times—once aloud, once to himself, and then aloud once more. Listening more carefully as Yakov read it a second time, Grisha couldn't help but be envious of his fellow dragons. It was true that they were far from home, but they had each other's company. Even though the threat of being sent to Siberia hung over them, they were alive.

It seemed to Grisha that waiting for jobs and registration, whatever that was, meant that Vienna's dragons had the chance to become part of the human world once again. He wasn't even a hundred and fifty years old. If it weren't for the teapot, he could go to Vienna and have a chance at his own adventure.

For the next week or two, Yakov was rarely home before midnight. He told Esther he was working late, and when he finally did return, the girls told him that he smelled of wet leaves and candy. Finally, Yakov came home at his normal time on a night when the girls and Esther were out.

Grisha, acutely aware of all sounds, could hear Yakov eating cheese and toast in the kitchen, and then hunting around until he returned with the old blackout curtains. He hung them in the front room where he normally wrote his letters, and locked the door. From deep within his briefcase, he took out a small, dark-green bottle made of glass. It had an elaborate top of brilliant, almost blinding crystal surrounding a cork.

Yakov put the bottle on his desk and proceeded to make, on top of the old coal stove, the syrupy coffee he loved.

Grisha, on the desk with the bottle, recognized it as a smaller version of the bottle that contained the morning potion. He watched as Yakov boiled his coffee, poured it into a small china cup, and carried it back to the table, where he sat drinking and looking at Grisha.

When his cup was empty, Yakov leaned forward. "Well, my friend, I don't know if you can hear me. I've always liked to think you could, but perhaps it has simply been my fancy."

Grisha, somewhat obviously, said nothing, and Yakov continued.

"You were my companion before I met Esther, and my children have loved you. I used to worry about where in the world you would go if you were free, but at last I have hope of an answer. They'll know what to do with you in Vienna."

He picked up the small glass bottle and said, "I've been to a chemist, and together we've tinkered with the potion I bought in Istanbul. We think filling you with hot water, nettles, and this newer potion will undo whatever spell put you into your current state."

Grisha could hardly believe what he was hearing. He'd spent almost a hundred years longing and wishing to be free, but not ever believing it could happen. Flashing across his unmoving gold eyes, he saw decades in the unhappy palace and the years in the shop window. He saw twenty-odd years in London that were happy, but marked by imprisonment.

And now here was Yakov talking about undoing Leopold Lashkovic's spell. It was hard to grasp. And, even as it was happening, it was almost impossible to believe.

Yakov boiled hot water, nettles, and the potion, filling the room with the smells of licorice and salty seaweed from the ocean. He poured the mixture into the teapot and then put him on the floor, after moving the chairs, desk, and ottoman out of the way.

For an hour or so, nothing happened. Grisha, remembering how Leopold Lashkovic had spoken the language of spells when turning him into a teapot, wondered whether a spell was what was missing. At just that moment, his scales tightened as if he needed to sneeze. And sneeze he did.

It was loud, deep, and forceful, like a cannon booming across a battlefield. It was as if the sneeze from so long ago, back when Leopold's powder had attacked Grisha's nose, eyes, and paw pads, had finally found its way out. The melting, bubbling, and dissolving feeling returned, along with a searing pain in his belly and his head.

Grisha's muscles uncoiled as unpolished gold made way for scales in shades of green, brown, and orange. Rubies vanished and a hot haze of smoke hung about the room as decades of fiery breath poured from Grisha's mouth. His wings unfurled and his feet wiggled; they were unbearably happy to be moving. His tail, which had been forced into the curve of a handle, blissfully thumped itself into fullness, knocking over everything that happened to be in its path.

Yakov was so excited that he grabbed hold of one of Grisha's paws. "My friend, how good to meet you. Welcome back to the world."

"We've met," Grisha told him. "I've known you all these years." He felt warmth and life flooding through his body from where his paw touched his friend's hand.

"Yes, yes, of course," Yakov said. "Tell me, what do they call you?"

"Grisha," Grisha said. "I am Grisha, short for Benevolentia Gaudium."

Yakov laughed and threw his arms around Grisha. Outside, a church bell rang out ten times.

"How did you do it?" Grisha asked. "I hope you didn't have to give up anything too precious." He hated to think that he had caused Yakov to give away time, money, or something he loved.

"Magic demands that you give up what you love. It's the simplest art and the most difficult to practice," Yakov said. "But with a potion, all you do is find the right one and use it."

Grisha was sure that wasn't true, but didn't want to press as Yakov seemed nervous. His friend was adjusting his cuffs, which did not need any adjusting. Grisha himself was nervous, worried that if Leopold were still alive, he might sense that one of his spells had been reversed and come looking for revenge. A sorcerer was always connected to his magic; he lost strength and power when any spell he'd cast came undone. Sometimes the only way a sorcerer could weaken or kill an enemy sorcerer was to reverse his rival's biggest spells.

"What do you eat?" Yakov asked. "I fear you must be starving."

"Well, I am rather hungry," Grisha said. His body was warming up and starting to make its needs and wishes known. Thoughts of Leopold and his magic vanished as the demands of being alive came into focus. "Do you have any acorns? Or even pinecones?"

There was nothing Grisha liked to eat less than a pinecone, but he was so hungry he knew he'd be happy to eat anything.

Yakov didn't have any, of course. But he made a big plate of mashed cabbage, potato, and apple and poured hot mulled cider over it. Grisha almost wept with pleasure. It had been over a hundred years since he'd had a meal. Food, he decided, was one of life's great joys along with the ability to move and breathe.

"We have to get you to Vienna," Yakov said. "Can you fit on a train?"

"I can scale to any size, but I have wings," Grisha said. "It's been a long time, but with some practice, I should be able to fly there."

"How much practice?" Yakov asked.

"I don't know," Grisha said. "I've never flown to Vienna after being trapped in a teapot before."

Yakov started to laugh. "I suppose you haven't."

"How soon must I be in Vienna?" Grisha asked.

"As soon as possible," Yakov said. "My uncle said they'll ship any dragon stragglers to Siberia."

"Please tell the girls how much I wanted to meet them," Grisha said. "And Esther."

Yakov nodded and said, "Go to the house where they stayed during the Blitz. You can practice and rest there." He rolled out a map and Grisha laughed.

"I don't need a map," he said. "It will smell like the girls."

"Could you smell when you were a teapot?" Yakov asked. "If I'd known that, I would have brought leaves from the forest to make you feel more at home."

Grisha was touched. "I couldn't smell in there, but I can now," he said. "Of the four human smells in the house, two have more strength. It means that they belong to youth."

Yakov still looked concerned. "Are you sure I shouldn't go with you?"

"I'll be all right on my own," Grisha said. "I promise."

"Of course," Yakov said. "Of course."

He and Grisha stared at each other, not knowing how to say either goodbye or thank you.

"Perhaps you will come to Vienna," Grisha said. "And we can see each other."

Yakov cleared his throat and wiped his eyes. "Wherever you go, you'll take a part of my heart," he told the dragon.

Grisha knew the reason he still had a heart after so long under Leopold Lashkovic's spell was entirely due to Yakov and the whole Merdinger family. He knew he would never forget them, even as he stepped outside into the city's gritty air and let his wings soar him back toward his true dragon self. He scaled up in size to match the strength his wings needed for flight. Breath moved effortlessly in and out of his lungs and through his mouth.

The higher up and the farther away from London he got, the more Grisha grasped that, at long last, he was able to move, to breathe, and to *be*. He was, once again, truly alive.

# CHAPTER SIX

# VIENNA

TEN DAYS OF REST IN THE ENGLISH COUNTRYSIDE
and a number of excellent meals consisting of acorns,
twigs, and leaves helped Grisha and his wings easily make
their way to Austria. Dragons always aim for water at the
end of long trips. Any flight over three hours makes their
breath heat up to such a degree that their blood starts to
simmer. The heated blood makes scales feel like burning
hot sand, and so cooling off is key. Which meant that
Grisha aimed his landing in the Danube.

After splashing around for a bit, Grisha made the
short flight to Vienna. There he found dragons in all of
the city's fine hotels, just as Yakov's uncle had written.
The soldiers assigned him to a room at the Bristol Hotel,
where he immediately spoke to the first dragon he'd seen
since leaving the forest.

"I don't know you, but your scent tells me I should," boomed a large, imposing dragon standing in the lobby. "You've a very peculiar smell, but there's a hint of the Breg under that aroma."

The Breg was one of the two small rivers deep in the Black Forest that crossed each other exactly where the Danube began. It pleased Grisha that a bit of the forest's smell had stuck with him after all these years.

"I grew up near the Breg," the imposing dragon said. "I suspect you did as well."

"I did, yes, hello!" Grisha said. "I'm Benevolentia Gaudium, but please use Grisha. Apologies for the peculiar smell. I was an enchantment for many years."

"Indomitus Ignis, but please, I am known as Kator," Kator said.

The two dragons bowed and then touched tails, which was how dragons who were meeting for the first time behaved. When not on the battlefield, dragons are exceedingly polite.

"I'm older than you, but only by seventy or so years," Kator informed Grisha.

The older a dragon was, the longer his tail's tip became. Each added inch reflected thirty-three years, and Kator's was two inches and a smidge longer than Grisha's.

"Maybe that's why I don't know you," Grisha said.

"That, and the world of magic sent me out to fight in the world of men when I was very young, and so I hardly even knew the dragons my own age," Kator said. "Until recently, I had never lost a fight."

For those of you interested, Indomitus Ignis means "ferocious fire." Kator had more than lived up to his name and had fought in many a battle. As a young dragon, Kator said, he'd even been chosen to serve as a protector of four enchanted cats. Kator reminded Grisha of the young dragons who'd bragged about all of the battles they would fight when they grew. However, this spirited, battle-scarred dragon with a splash of black along his neck already had done many marvelous things worth boasting about.

Kator took it upon himself to introduce Grisha to the other dragons in the city. Not all of them were from the Black Forest, and each was older than Grisha. He bowed with everyone and learned that the dragons who'd fought in Japan preferred not to touch tails, but left front paws. The dragons all commented on his peculiar smell, but were welcoming. It was good to be among his own kind as he slowly adjusted to his new life in Vienna.

Even without Kator pointing it out, Grisha understood that much had changed in both the world of magic and that of men. Dragons had once been part of how people brought magic into the world, but now the world, it was plain to see, had no use for either. Both the soldiers and the city's people ate, spoke, thought, and moved faster than seemed possible to Grisha. Anything or anyone that threatened to be time-consuming but not immediately important was pushed aside. American and British soldiers, having been put in charge of sorting out all of Europe's refugee trouble, treated the dragons not as fellow warriors, but as problems involving no solution and too much paperwork.

While the dragons didn't think of themselves as a problem, they knew that being in Vienna was problematic. The challenges that had started with the steam engine, railways, and light bulbs had, with the passage of time, become impossibly difficult facts of life. There were lights everywhere, even at night, and people behaved as if the sun never set. The dragons developed severe eyestrain. Their small, sensitive ears, while used to blocking out battle sounds, were totally unprepared for the din of modern daily life.

Much to their embarrassment, the dragons found themselves so stressed that they frequently lost control over when they would exhale flames instead of air. The curtains in the Bristol's front dining room caught fire often. Watching the soldiers douse the curtains with water for a third time, Grisha asked Kator why on earth he and the others had left the forest. "I came here because Yakov said this was where the dragons were," Grisha reminded him. "But you were safely at home."

"There was a sound in the forest that called us to follow it," Kator said. "It sounded like the leaves moving or a stream rushing, and it carried a clear message: Either we left the forest immediately for Vienna, or we would find ourselves in northern Siberia."

Northern Siberia is a vast stretch of land that is all ice and chill and freeze. Dragons in exile there would not only be cold and hungry, but hopelessly isolated. They would all die of starvation or frostbite. It would be far worse than life in the teapot, Grisha thought, and was glad he hadn't heard the sound.

"It's so strange," Kator told him. "The sound made us rush to the city, but when we got to Vienna, it was clear no one wanted us here."

Grisha looked at the tattered remains of the once-elegant curtains and said, "It's hard to blame people who think we're a nuisance."

It was right around then that Kator pointed out to everyone that no new dragon had been born since the year of Grisha's birth. At a hundred and forty-odd years, Grisha was the youngest dragon in Vienna.

"Our time, like that of magic itself, has come and gone," Lennox said. He was the eldest amongst them and their unofficial leader. He was almost entirely silver, which was a color few dragons ever turned, as most of them died in battle well before their four-hundredth birthdays.

When he and Grisha had touched tails in greeting, Lennox had sniffed deeply as if wanting to figure out where the strange dragon was from. "I was sorry to hear of your troubles," he'd said. "I fought side by side with your father once. Although he was very young I could see greatness in him."

Lennox was no longer as strong as he once had been, but his voice was still a typical military-sounding mix of thunder and trumpets, even when he kept it soft and low. "We will end our days in this strange city," he continued now.

Grisha didn't like the sound of that. To end one's days surely meant Lennox thought the dragons would all die in Vienna. If that were true, then Grisha very much wanted to see his forest again and drink from the small streams that crossed where the Danube began.

"Can we ever go home?" Grisha asked.

"They have guns," Kator said, meaning the soldiers who kept watch over them.

"And they are willing to use them outside of battle," Lennox said. "So we can do nothing they will not allow."

Grisha, who had never heard of a dragon facing down a gun in the world of men unless on the battlefield, had quizzed Kator on why the soldiers were so quick to threaten to shoot. "We're in a hotel," Grisha had said to his friend. He was deeply puzzled about why a soldier had pointed a gun at him to keep him from leaving the hotel. "We aren't fighting them, but they'd shoot us for being in the wrong place at the wrong time?"

Kator had taken him back to their room and tried to answer. He told Grisha of changes that had happened in the forest even before the last war. It wasn't simply the steam engine and the railways. "Men were everywhere in the forest, but not for hunting," he explained. "They cut down trees! So many trees were killed, and then they built houses and stores."

It was sad enough when a tree died from disease or lightning, Grisha thought. He was even more heartsick at the thought of so many beloved trees dying at the hands of an ax. "We had to hide all the time, because the men shot to kill whenever they saw one of us," Kator said.

"But there was no battle," Grisha said. He couldn't quite believe it.

"We thought it was because they weren't soldiers or hunters and didn't understand about the rules of a fair fight," Kator said. "But they shot us simply because we existed."

When the dragons arrived in Vienna, Kator explained, the soldiers had let it be known that if the fire-breathing creatures refused to obey orders, they would be shot. The days of fair fighting between the world of magic and the world of men was over.

"Isn't it dangerous for us now that none of the old rules apply?" Grisha asked.

"Dragons were created because life *is* dangerous," Kator said. "I'm more worried that none of the soldiers fear anything at all."

Grisha wasn't sure if that was true, but he knew his friend had far more experience with all things military. He understood that the other dragons were full of resentments and grudges toward the soldiers because of their guns, but Grisha tended to feel sorry for them. They were such young men—younger than Yakov had been when he'd purchased Grisha—and they seemed just as confused and frightened as he himself was.

After all, although it was wise to fear a human with a gun, Grisha had spent his captivity observing humans and their sometimes odd behaviors. His habit of observation allowed him to see past the guns and the uniforms. He could tell that the soldiers were homesick, as well as scared of the lumbering, fire-breathing beasts in their charge. They meant well without knowing what to do. So Grisha tried to understand them as best he could.

Over several days, he repeatedly heard the soldiers discussing a man who was coming to solve everything by his processing. "What do they mean by 'processing'?" Grisha asked one night in the Bristol's dining room, where the dragons sat hunched over meager plates of wilted lettuce.

"It means there are too many of us," Lennox said. Too many of us for what, Grisha wondered.

The answer was made most horribly clear when the man whom the soldiers had been waiting for finally arrived. There were too many dragons, it turned out, for all of them to be free.

>—•—<

The man who arrived in Vienna did not belong to the world of men, but to what remained of magic. His magic had diminished over the years, and he'd grown bitter over the way his powers were no longer in high demand. He was determined to show these soldiers that he could do what they could not. Perhaps he was older and weaker than he once had been, but he still had more power than the soldiers with their many guns.

The man saw at once that there were too many dragons for the city. So he divided them into two groups: those with gold eyes and those without. Grisha, Kator, Lennox, and about thirty-five others had gold eyes, so they were each assigned a job and a place to call home, a warm bed, and food to eat. The jobs were simple, but designed to give the city's historical buildings an interesting addition. Museum dragons found lost children, palace dragons guarded jewels, and others made sure to report needed repairs in old yet still grand buildings.

The seventy-five or so dragons with violet, red, or brown eyes did not get homes, beds, food, or even jobs. Instead, the dragons without gold eyes were nowhere to be found. They were alive, but victims of an enchantment far worse than being trapped in a teapot.

For almost a year, the luckier golden-eyed dragons brooded and worried about what had happened to the other dragons. But soon enough they decided it was best to focus on what was good in their new lives, and not on what had gone wrong. The forest had taught them to stay alive, and sometimes forgetting what was unpleasant was the best way to live.

At least, Grisha thought, every dragon who'd come to Vienna still was alive.

Grisha was assigned to live and work in one of the most beautiful and decrepit castles on the Danube. At first, he tried hard to remember the fate of the unlucky dragons. After all, he knew too well what it was like to be unlucky. Eventually, however, he too felt forced to accept that there was nothing he could do to change what had happened. Soon, he no longer thought about it. Instead, he let a fog grow over the memories of his first year in Vienna.

Anxious to put all reminders of a destructive, cruel, and violent war behind them, the city and its people also forgot.

# CHAPTER SEVEN

# GIRL IN A CITY

**ABOUT FORTY YEARS AFTER THE DRAGONS ARRIVED** in Vienna, a girl child was born there. These days, of course, a girl child's birth is a common event. However, as this girl grew, she refused to ignore what her city had forgotten. As a result, we must thank her for all that is known about Vienna's dragons.

For the girl, Vienna was not simply a place, but an old friend who helped raise her. She was a city child through and through; until she was eleven, she had never seen or walked through a forest.

In the strange and mysterious ways of grown-ups everywhere, her parents named the girl Anna Marguerite, but agreed to call her Maggie. These particular parents, Alexander Miklós and Caroline Brooks, had never planned to have a baby, just as they had never planned to fall in love or marry. Each of them, before meeting the other, would have told you that getting married and having children was a plan only for other sorts of people. Not for a famous poet (Maggie's father) or an even more famous painter (her mother).

And yet somehow it had happened, in the strange and mysterious way that it often does.

>—•—<

One day when Maggie was three, her mother, the tall, beautiful, and talented Caroline Brooks, packed a bag and caught a train out of the city. There was a gallery in Germany that was showing her paintings. She planned to be back in two days, she told Maggie, and with chocolates.

On that brisk, sunny morning, Caroline hugged her daughter, kissed her husband, and left for Berlin, confident that she would see them again soon.

But in Berlin, there was a car crash, and Caroline Brooks died immediately. Not the sort of thing that anyone had planned for.

Alexander Miklós was now a famous poet and a man who would have to raise his daughter alone. And Maggie was now a child with no memory whatsoever of her mother. This was, Maggie felt, the worst part of the car crash. It was practically impossible to miss someone you couldn't remember.

Whenever the topic of Caroline came up, Maggie was uncomfortable, as if she had done something wrong to be the sort of child incapable of missing her mother. She missed the *idea* of a mother, and that idea was formed from storybooks or by watching other children with their mothers. She'd glimpse a woman wiping a child's face and wonder if her own mother had ever done that.

Maggie had seen so many women grab the hand of a child crossing the street that she assumed that Caroline had done the same at some point. But maybe not, for Alexander always had preferred to put his hand on her shoulder and murmur, *Look both ways first.*

She supposed she could ask her father: *What kind of mother was she?* After all, he believed in having a curious mind, and repeatedly said that there was no such thing as a stupid question, or one too small. But even seven years after her mother's death, Maggie could see her father's eyes tighten and his jaw stiffen if anyone mentioned Caroline. It was all right if he mentioned her first, but it was clearly upsetting if anyone else did. Maggie refused to cause him any pain just from curiosity about a woman she neither missed nor remembered.

Alexander often said that over time Maggie would come to know her mother through her paintings. Maggie thought, but did not say, that looking at paintings was not the best way to know a parent.

Caroline had been a loving mother for three years, but Maggie knew her only from photos. Or by what other people said. And people said a lot, but they mostly whispered things like *Poor dear* and *So unfortunate* and, most irritatingly, *Such a plain child, yet the mother was a great beauty.* Maggie didn't think it should matter very much if she were plain or if her mother had been a great beauty. Her mother, beautiful or not, was dead.

*Wonder if she has the mother's talent, poor dear* was another whisper Maggie often heard. She herself did not wonder, as she had seen her own drawings and understood that they were terrible. *Actually, the poor dear doesn't,* Maggie longed to say in reply, but her father believed that being polite wasn't simply about manners, but kindness.

"Rude words make everything worse," he'd say. "Try and be kind."

So no matter how irritated the whispered comments made her, Maggie never spoke up. She thought it was enough that she knew about her own lack of talent. In her sketches, no matter how careful she was, her figures were always potato-like lumps trying to be something other than potatoes.

As a rule, people do not enjoy doing things poorly, and Maggie was no exception. She would never be a painter and she had no wish to be a poet. While she knew her father loved his work, reading his poems often felt like using a very confusing map.

She liked to read, but knew she'd never enjoy a life spent at a desk. Her father sat countless hours at his, hunched over ink-stained papers or staring out of the window. Sometimes Maggie saw him simply staring into space as if he could see what no one else could.

"I'm not staring," he told her once. "I'm either thinking or trying to think."

"Doesn't thinking just happen?" Maggie asked. For her it did, and she didn't think she was doing it wrong.

"Yes, but when you're writing a poem, thinking doesn't always happen the way you want it to," Alexander said. "So I stare because I'm trying to understand my thoughts."

Maggie nodded as if she understood him perfectly. But all she really understood was that her father sat at his desk. A lot.

So she didn't try writing a poem to discover if she was as bad at poetry as she was at painting. It was one thing to muck about with charcoal, paint, and paper. At least that was a bit fun. Sit down and *try* to think? That was not for Maggie, who preferred walking to sitting, and thinking to *trying* to think.

She didn't mind sitting and reading, and would often do that by her father's desk while he worked. Which was not to say that he worked so much that he had no time for Maggie. Alexander, in spite of never having planned to be a father, let alone a single parent, turned out to be a really great one. He had seen right away that if he was going to be in charge of Maggie's basic requirements (meals, clean clothes, tidy rooms, and safe places to play), he would probably need some help.

Before Caroline's death, Maggie had spent most of her time at home, in her mother's art studio, or with a nanny. The art studio was now empty and Alexander had fired the nanny, whom he'd never liked. On a few occasions, he took Maggie to his office at the University of Vienna, where he was a professor, but that was neither fun nor safe for a little girl. She used his entire collection of poetry books to build a fort, and when she ran out of books she wandered into other people's offices to find more. She only succeeded in annoying everyone and making a mess. Plus, when she'd tried to pet the cat who'd made a home in the poetry and literature offices, it had scratched her across the face. Four stitches, but no permanent scar.

So Alexander sold their apartment and rented a few rooms at the Hotel Sacher. The hotel took care of meals, clean clothes, and tidy rooms. She and her father settled happily into their new, if somewhat unusual, home.

Whenever Alexander had to be at the university, he hired one of his students to take Maggie out or one of the hotel staff to stay inside with her. In this way, both the hotel lobby and the city itself became playrooms where she could make a mess without annoying others. Nor could she cause herself any harm.

When Maggie was old enough to go to school, Alexander enrolled her in one and then, just as quickly, took her out. He was horrified by the rules that served no purpose and the boring nature of the schoolwork. She came home one day with a teacher's note saying that a book he'd given her to read was inappropriate for a child. He threw the note away—and that turned out to be Maggie's last day at school.

If Alexander had needed help keeping his daughter fed, clean, and safe, he most certainly didn't need help to teach her. She had lessons in the morning at home with her father, and while he taught her math, Latin, German, English, and history on a daily basis, he also made sure to teach her whatever she found interesting.

There was only one small gap in her education: Maggie had no idea how to make friends.

She *saw* friends everywhere in Vienna. People her age playing in a park or walking home in small groups after school. In the cafés, she saw old men arguing while playing chess, or young men laughing loudly over coffee and cake. She saw women talking on the streetcars and sidewalks and in parks and cafés. They talked and talked and talked, yet Maggie never overheard anything that sounded important enough for so much discussion.

Talking seemed to be the key to all the friendships she saw, and Alexander himself talked (as well as laughed and argued) when he was with his friends. Maggie could talk in almost three languages. Her best was English, which she and her father spoke at home; then German, which she spoke with everyone else; and some French, which she studied when her father thought she'd practiced enough German for the week.

If talking is all it takes, I can make friends, she thought. She was quite confident, but quickly discovered that something else was necessary. Whatever it was, she was missing it.

The year she was eight, she tried several times to talk with kids she saw in the park. Prepared to use her best German, she approached a group playing football and said, "How do you do?"

The children, three boys and two girls aged about eight to ten, stopped what they were doing and stared at her. Maggie wondered if she shouldn't introduce herself. "I'm Anna Marguerite, which is a little silly, so people call me Maggie."

"Do you play?" asked one of the girls, although she spoke very quickly, so it sounded like "Dojyaplài?"

Maggie was quiet for a bit longer than the group considered normal. *Dojyaplài?* Her mind was sounding it out.

"You deaf?" one of the boys asked loudly and slowly.

"Oh!" she exclaimed. *Do you play!* Got it. "No, I'm not," she said to the boy.

She considered which German verb tense would best explain to the girl that she had often wished to play football. Maggie had imagined playing it so often that she thought she could play really well. In fact, she was dying to race across the park, keeping the ball safely between her feet while also magically letting it get ahead of her. But by the time she looked up with a detailed, perfectly composed answer, the group had run off and was playing in the distance.

The next time, she sought out a different group and had a well-prepared answer to *Do you play?* but no one asked if she could. One of the kids said yes, her name was rather silly, and another wanted to know where she lived.

"The Hotel Sacher," Maggie said.

"Why do you live in a hotel?" a girl about Maggie's age asked. They smiled briefly at each other.

"That's weird," one of the boys said. "No one lives in a hotel."

"It *is* weird," another boy said.

Now Maggie was nervous in a way that had nothing to do with German verb tenses. "My father is the poet Alexander Miklós, and he thought it best," she said. Her chest was tight and her arms gripped against her sides. She could hear how stiff and unpleasant her voice was, but she couldn't make herself use polite, friendly tones.

"*You're* weird," the first boy said.

Perhaps if Maggie had been at school surrounded all day by other children, she might have known to shrug and laugh. But while she had often heard people talk about her dead mother, her famous father, and her own plain looks, no one had ever before said anything unkind directly to her.

"You're very rude," she said. "I don't think I care to know you."

All of the kids began laughing, and the girl Maggie had smiled at called her a weirdo. The German, *verrückter Typ*, made it sound even worse.

>—•—<

As she grew, Maggie began to understand that the way she and her father lived was not considered normal. It wasn't simply living in a hotel that people found so strange. It was that Alexander wanted her to study whatever she liked best, to develop independent thoughts, and to play freely. When other grown-ups described Maggie's education, they used words like *unusual* and *odd*, *questionable* and *judgment*.

But Maggie enjoyed spending her days learning about what interested her. If she liked something, Alexander bought her books or took her to see what it was that had caught her attention. As a result, she learned a great deal—

about Europe's wars (for she loved swords and cannons); kings, queens, and emperors (palaces and jewelry); and how stained glass was made (cathedral windows).

Maggie much preferred her afternoons with hotel staff, who were willing to do jigsaw puzzles or play games with her, to those spent with Alexander's graduate students, who were only interested in discussing her father or poetry. But she appreciated that because of them, she could go anywhere she wanted in the city.

What she liked to do most was get on a streetcar and ride it to its end. Sometimes, she'd want to search a new neighborhood for a *Konditorei* that had the best-looking display of cakes. Sometimes she'd want to walk all the way home from a new neighborhood. Or, if the weather was poor, she'd happily ride the streetcars in any direction at all.

Riding the streetcars in this random manner drove the graduate students crazy, and the greatest moment of Maggie's young life was when she turned nine and Alexander decided that she could go out on her own wherever she pleased and do as she liked. Every Monday morning, he gave her a weekly pass for Vienna's buses, streetcars, and subways, which were called the *U-Bahn*.

While she was delighted to be free of her father's poetry-obsessed students, Maggie found that she missed having someone with whom she could share her discoveries or observations. Silly things, like *This Konditorei has the best almond cake*, but also somewhat more serious matters. Like when she was forced to acknowledge that she had walked so far from the tram stop that she was lost. Her German was good enough to ask a stranger the best way back to the last streetcar she'd been on, but being lost embarrassed her. Vienna was her own city, after all. What sort of ridiculous person got lost in her own city?

After being hopelessly turned around and not at all certain of the way back, Maggie came to see that getting lost just meant discovering a new way to get home. By the sixth time this happened, she knew not to panic, to try and find her way to a familiar landmark, or to ask an older person as politely as possible for directions. She was always glad to get home, but mostly Maggie was happy to know that, thanks to her father's *questionable judgment* plus his *unusual* and *odd* ideas about education, she had learned both how to get lost and how to find her own way.

# CHAPTER EIGHT

# Is It Fun?

For her eleventh birthday, Alexander gave in to Maggie's begging to stay up late with him in the evenings. That was when he met his friends at the Blaue Bar. The bar was in the hotel lobby, and where Maggie often had lunch if Alexander had to be at the university earlier than normal. Sometimes she would just wander in and nibble from the dishes of nuts. Every so often, Kurt, the old bartender, would let her help cut up the lemons and limes.

According to Alexander, Maggie had taken her first steps in the Blaue Bar one night while he and Caroline were having cake and coffee at the end of a long day. Maggie had no memory of that, of course, and simply loved the bar because it was beautiful. Dark blue velvet covered the chairs and the bar stools. Even the walls were covered in light blue velvet with gold overleaf on which hung burnished lamps.

Alexander met his friends there very late every evening, after the Opera was done, so that the singers could join the city's painters, sculptors, musicians, and poets. They were the sorts of people who liked to talk and smoke and argue about things Maggie found hard to understand. But she liked how excited they all got about their discussion.

That wasn't, however, why she wanted to stay up late in the bar. One reason was because she hated how, as soon as she fell asleep upstairs, Alexander left their rooms to go downstairs. She wanted to be included in this part of her father's life.

But the main reason Maggie wanted to be at the Blaue Bar late at night was the dragons. Once a week, at around two in the morning, a group of the city's dragons gathered at the bar, laughing and talking. Even though Maggie had now lived at the hotel for seven years, she'd only ever seen them there twice. They would loudly ask Kurt to bring them pitchers of fermented *Apfelsaft*, which was, as far as Maggie could tell, apple juice mixed with vinegar. It smelled so terrible that she could not bring herself to even try it, but she loved watching the dragons stand around the bar, jostling each other for position.

When she started coming to the bar every night with her father, she tried to stay up, but usually fell asleep next to him on the blue velvet banquette or curled underneath the table. The floor was covered in a beautiful soft rug and the heavy marble table made a canopy, blocking out light and sound. Almost every week, she missed the dragons because she was asleep.

Finally, one night the dragons were still there when her father woke her. Maggie wondered how it was that twenty dragons could fit in the small Blaue Bar when the ones she had seen elsewhere in the city were almost as big as the bar itself.

"They scale to size," Alexander told her. "That way they are never too big or too small to fit with their surroundings."

When getting into her warm bed as the sun was beginning its rise, Maggie would think how lucky she was to live in Vienna, where the world's last dragons lived, and to have a father who let her see every bit of the city, no matter the hour.

·

Over the years, Grisha had come to love his new home. It wasn't his forest or, for that matter, any forest, but he was, at long last, a flesh-and-blood dragon again. If not as free as he'd been before Leopold's spell, he was far freer than he'd dared to hope while he was a teapot. His castle had plenty of sunny spots, and the people who visited were thrilled to have a dragon there to answer their questions.

He and Kator, who lived in another castle on the Danube, often visited each other. They would sit and sun themselves or, on cold, rainy days, watch the slate-gray river go by and talk. They were careful not to talk too much of home or their early years in Vienna, but Kator had a lot of battle stories. Between those stories and the ones of people Grisha saw at his castle, they always had something to discuss.

"How do you notice these things?" Kator asked, after Grisha recounted a story about a woman whose open purse revealed a water bottle, an umbrella, a sweater, Band-Aids, paper napkins, and a very mashed piece of cake.

"I've had lots of practice watching people," Grisha said. "You could do the same at your castle."

"People only interest me on the battlefield," Kator said. "Off of it, I much prefer the company of dragons."

Kator was not alone in this sentiment. All the dragons loved the weekly gatherings at the Hotel Sacher. Grisha found these nights to be precious beyond all others. He only wished that the dragons could meet at a more reasonable hour than two in the morning. It wasn't that he was tired then (created by magic for battle, dragons needed very little sleep), but he loved watching the city's sky in the hours before sunrise. When you have lived most of your life as a prisoner, you come to crave the outside as if it were the best chocolate in the world.

However, two in the morning it was, as the Department of Extinct Exotics—known as the D.E.E.—had made an agreement with the hotel manager that the dragons would not come until the bar was closed to the general public. The D.E.E. was tasked with overseeing the dragons' lives and controlling their interactions with the general population.

In Vienna, dragons were a fact of city life, as basic as streetcars and rude waiters. They hardly ever scared anyone and often people were simply too busy to notice them. But the hotel's manager didn't want to take a chance that one of their out-of-town guests would wander in and be terrified. It was one thing for a tourist to look forward to seeing a dragon walking through a palace or giving directions in a museum and quite another to see one unexpectedly in a hotel.

Thus the late hour for the weekly gathering of dragons was arranged so that the bar would be empty. However, when Grisha and his friends arrived, there were often people still at a large table in the back. According to the bartender, they were all of Vienna's artists.

"None of them are sensible enough to be scared of you lot," he said.

"No one is scared of us anymore," Kator said, sounding both sad and confused.

Annoushka, a dragon who had once held an entire army at bay for five months in order to save a queen locked up in a tower, joined in. "If only the law allowed," she said, "I would teach everyone how to fear us." When she grinned, Annoushka revealed several broken teeth, a sure sign that she had removed swords from men with a single bite.

Grisha, who had never wanted anyone to be afraid of him, returned to watching the people at the table. The opera singers were loud, the artists had paint on their shoes, and the poets were quiet. There was sometimes a young girl sound asleep under the table. She looked like a tangle of arms and legs that had collapsed in utter exhaustion. He noticed that her brown hair had usually slipped away from a poorly tied ribbon.

On one particularly cold and wet February night the girl woke up, untangled herself from under the table, and wandered over to the bar. She moved as if her body were graceful and clumsy in equal parts. She had large brown eyes full of quiet observation and she was neither beautiful nor plain. Instead, her long face looked as if it might break into either a giggle or a yawn at any moment.

Since most of the dragons were busy boasting about their amazing deeds, only Grisha noticed the girl. Of all the people who came through his castle to climb the turrets and descend into the dungeons, the children were his favorites. They never asked boring questions like "In what year was this structure built?" or "Which king was it that the emperor held prisoner?" Instead, children wanted to know where people who'd lived in the castle had gone to the bathroom (outside) or how many soldiers could fit into the turret (Grisha had no idea, but always said seven, an answer that seemed to satisfy, although one girl had insisted it must be thirteen).

This girl, however, did not seem like the insisting type, so Grisha introduced himself and asked her name.

Maggie hesitated, remembering the last time she had told a stranger her name.

"I'm Anna Marguerite, which is a little silly," she said. "So people call me Maggie."

"It's not at all silly," Grisha said, and was rewarded by a huge smile. "Grisha is short for Benevolentia Gaudium."

"Kindness and joy!" Maggie exclaimed, happy to encounter Latin outside of a book. "How does Grisha come from that?"

"It just does," he said.

"Well, it *is* shorter," she said.

They looked at each other shyly, each happy to have met the other, but not sure that the other person (or dragon) wanted to be bothered.

"Would you like to eat?" Grisha asked. "Are you hungry?"

He knew that the Blaue Bar had a late-night menu and that people, unlike dragons, often ate their meals together (dragons crave company, but rarely enjoy eating with one another).

"Oh, yes, I'm starved," Maggie said. "Do you think I could get some strudel?"

Grisha asked the waiter to bring a plate of warm strudel with whipped cream as well as a mug of hot chocolate, for he was under the impression that human children liked to drink that. He was also under the impression that human children did not fall asleep under hotel tables unless they had a grown-up with them.

"Which one belongs to you?" Grisha asked, looking at the group of Vienna's artists, who were all talking, laughing, arguing, drinking, and eating.

"With the pipe," Maggie said, pointing to a tall man in a tweed jacket. "He's my papa, but you would call him Alexander."

Alexander was listening to several people at once. He also had a long, serious face that looked, Grisha thought, like it had fallen out of the habit of smiling. That is the sort of thing dragons see, although they are never sure if they are right. People are odd creatures and sometimes they cry when they are happy, so it can be hard to tell if what you see is what you think it is. Even if you are a dragon who has decades of practice watching people.

"He's a very famous poet," Maggie said. She said this matter-of-factly, as if stating that he was tall or busy or at the dentist.

"I see," said Grisha. He was not at all surprised that someone's father was famous, as fame in the dragon world was a given. After all, each dragon was famous to all the others because of their particular battles, adventures, or exploits.

"If you know about things like poetry, that is," Maggie said.

"I don't know anything about poetry," Grisha said. "Is it fun?"

"Fun," Maggie repeated slowly. No one had ever asked her that before. Fun and poetry were words like "delicious" and "espresso," she thought. In theory, they could be one and the same, but it probably depended on the person. She tried to imagine her father's students having fun, but couldn't. "I'm not sure it's fun," she said. "Probably not."

"That's too bad," Grisha said. He was glad she'd given her answer some thought, for fun was not a topic to be treated lightly.

Even though they are born to spend their lives scaring people, guarding them, or haunting their dreams, dragons are deeply devoted to fun. When dragons boasted of their epic adventures, what they were really proclaiming was that their lives had been fun. It was an open secret in the world of magic that if the world of men had known to tell a joke or invent a game at crucial moments, a lot of famous battles would never have taken place. The dragons would have been entirely too distracted to fight.

The food came, and Grisha and Maggie carried it to one of the little tables right next to the bar. Maggie took a huge bite of strudel and then asked the waiter for extra whipped cream. "The only thing I like more than whipped cream is butter," she explained to Grisha after the waiter had said, *Certainly, miss.*

"So what do you do for fun?" she asked, once it had been established that he was not interested in having his own pastry.

"I nap in the sun," he said. "Or my friend Kator comes to visit." He pointed to the bar where Kator was talking.

"The one with the velvet covering his scales?" Maggie asked.

"Yes," Grisha said, impressed she had noticed a detail like that. "He claims that in one of his big battles a prince used a poisoned blade to burn away seventeen of his scales."

"But you don't believe him?"

"Well, when I first met him, he didn't have any velvet scales, so I am not sure."

"Why would anyone lie about that?" Maggie asked.

"It's not a lie, exactly, but a fake injury will make a battle story sound better," Grisha explained. "Dragons love a good story."

"He seems very loud," Maggie said. "Do you spend a lot of time with him?"

"He is much quieter when he and I are alone."

"That's good," Maggie said, sounding relieved. "Where do you live?"

Grisha told her about his castle, and Maggie said she would be very jealous if she weren't living in the hotel.

"This hotel?" Grisha asked her. "The Sacher?"

"Yes," she said.

"I didn't know people lived in hotels," he said. "I thought they stayed in them."

"Well, when my mother was alive, we all lived in an apartment," Maggie said.

Grisha, thinking of his own father, felt a sudden stab of sadness for the girl seated opposite him.

"It was behind the Rathauspark and City Hall," Maggie said. "I don't remember living there. I don't actually remember her either, but she was more famous than my papa."

Grisha knew how hard it was to have no memory of someone important from your life. The grief he'd felt when he discovered his mother had died while he was trapped in the teapot had been big and solid. The sadness about his father, of whom he had no memories, had been small and quiet, but just as real. What he missed, he'd discovered, was not the older dragon himself, but the chance to have known his father at all.

"I think the Sacher is an excellent place to call home," Grisha said gently.

He had been alive for a very long time and he knew when people wanted to talk and when they didn't. He understood that Maggie did not want to talk about her mother or the apartment or anything she didn't remember. It would be rude to ask about what wasn't any of his business. Dragons are not rude creatures.

It had gotten late and Alexander's friends were putting on their coats. At the bar, the dragons were finishing their stories. Soon it would be time for Grisha to return home to his castle on the Danube.

Alexander walked over to the table where Maggie and Grisha were sitting. Maggie introduced them, and Grisha, who didn't like to shake hands with humans (he worried his scales might scratch them), bowed in her father's direction. There were white hairs all along the hem of Alexander's trousers, as if a furry creature had been resting against him.

"Thank you for keeping my daughter amused," he said. "I fear my friends and I can be boring company for a little girl."

Grisha could see that Maggie did not like being referred to as a little girl, and so he quickly said, "She was amusing me. She was kind enough to keep me company while my companions all told stories I have heard many times already."

"Will I see you again next week?" Maggie asked Grisha.

"That would be very pleasant," Grisha said.

"You mustn't feel obliged," Alexander said. "I know I shouldn't let her stay up so late, but I can't bear to—"

"I don't feel obliged," Grisha said, interrupting, but wanting to be clear. "I very much meant that it would be very pleasant."

The dragons were beginning to make their way to the lobby. Alexander and Maggie walked with Grisha to the hotel's heavy front doors.

Maggie, in spite of having seen Grisha bow to her father, decided against such formality. She put her arms around as much of his middle as she could reach. Grisha remained as still as possible, not wanting to cause a rip in her pretty, if fairly mussed, velvet dress.

"Good night," she said, turning to take her father's outstretched hand.

The beginnings of dawn were creeping through the big windows on either side of the Sacher's front door. Grisha thought it was a very fine thing to have met such a charming girl. One with such serious eyes and who said good night just as the morning greeted you.

CHAPTER NINE

# STORIES

**MUCH TO GRISHA'S PLEASURE, HE WAS ABLE TO**
spend time with Maggie at the Blaue Bar the next week
and the one after that, and after that. She would be, as
always, sound asleep, but she had clearly arranged with
her father to wake her as soon as the dragons arrived.
Then she would greet Grisha and they would sit at a table
by the bar. Over hot chocolate with extra whipped cream
(for her) and fermented *Apfelsaft* (for him) they would
talk about their week and about what they knew or hoped
to know someday.

They gossiped about Alexander's friends crowded
around the back table and about the dragons at the bar.
Maggie would tell Grisha about the other children staying
at the hotel, invariably with two parents and on a holiday
from school. Grisha would tell Maggie about the children

who visited his castle and the large family of mice who lived in what was left of the crumbling dungeon.

One evening, they discovered that they each thought the Stadtpark was the most beautiful place in Vienna, but that Maggie had never been to it at night. Grisha, thinking that she would like to go, asked her father for permission to take her there.

"Just bring her back once she's seen the sun break through the trees," Alexander said.

"Yes, certainly," Grisha said, grateful that the poet understood how important it was to see the Stadtpark under its darkest sky, but also how it looked turning all of its early-morning colors.

Maggie led Grisha to her favorite corner of the park. It was the one from where she had once seen a large number of peacocks.

"They're not peacocks," Grisha said, surprised that she didn't know this. "They are descended from the children of winged horses and camels in Mongolia."

"How did they have babies that look like birds?" Maggie asked. "Wouldn't a winged horse and a camel have a baby that looked more like a horse?"

"It was a punishment," Grisha said. "The winged horses weren't supposed to be in Mongolia, and back when the world of magic had more power, it was against the rules for any of us to fall in love with any creature from the world of men."

"Why?" Maggie asked.

"Creatures from the world of magic were used whenever the world of men fought for power, not when men fought for love," Grisha said. "We went to the world of men to work with soldiers, not to fall in love."

"But soldiers fall in love," Maggie said. "Everyone does."

Grisha realized she'd never even seen a rabbit with a small black dot on each ear. Explaining magic, its rules, and how it was connected to the world of men was going to be hard. Maybe like trying to describe flying to someone without wings.

"It's different when love happens across two worlds," he said. "Bad things happen."

He told her how when a unicorn and a deer fell in love, hunters would invade the forest, intent on killing magical creatures.

"Oh, then the rule about love makes sense," Maggie said, wrapping her long arms around herself. "Papa thinks rules should only exist for physical protection. He says a rule that exists for any other purpose is the result of sloppy thinking."

Alexander had said exactly that on her last day of school. He'd had to explain why he allowed her to read anything she wanted, but wouldn't let her play with his Japanese sword.

"Are you cold?" Grisha asked, as she continued hugging herself.

"I am," she said, "but I don't want to leave."

The dragon went over to some nearby bushes and gathered some slender branches. He picked up a few stones from the pathway. In no time at all, and with just one well-placed breath, he had a small but steady fire going.

He scaled up in size a bit and curled his body around Maggie's bench. "Now I can block the wind," he said.

Together they sat in silence, watching for the sky to streak purple, pink, and pale blue as signs of the rising sun.

It had been almost forty years since Grisha had lived amongst humans, and until he met Maggie, he had not realized how much he had missed the company of a creature from the world of men.

Maggie, so long used to having only Alexander for company, was delighted to have a companion who hadn't been hired to take care of her. While listening to Grisha's breathing, she realized that he was her first friend. It's good that I didn't make any before, she thought. Playing football couldn't come close to how perfect it was to sit with Grisha and watch the sky.

>—•—<

One night—or rather one morning—just as Alexander was saying goodbye to his friends and the dragons were slipping away toward the lobby, Maggie asked Grisha why he never joined in any of the loud boasting at the bar about heroic and dastardly deeds.

"The others never stop talking and bragging," she said. "But you never start." She'd wondered about this for many weeks before deciding it was best to ask him.

"Well, I don't have a story," he said, fear entering his heart the way cold mornings crept through his Danube castle. He realized that over the past few months all thoughts of his teapot life had been banished while he enjoyed his new companion.

"Of course you have a story," she said. "Everyone does."

This was something Maggie had heard her father say many times. She had even read an article about her mother's career in which he was quoted as saying that Caroline's paintings didn't just show her story, but reminded everyone who looked at them what their own stories were.

"I'm not everyone," Grisha said, dreading her reaction. He pointed to the bar and said, "While they were all having adventures, I was trapped."

"Where?" Maggie asked. "When? How come? How long?"

Grisha had been expecting disappointment or boredom. Most of the dragons knew the bare details of his captivity, but none of them had ever expressed any interest in knowing more. Kator, in whom Grisha might have confided, had simply shuddered upon hearing the barest of details and said, "How very dull. I'm so sorry for you."

Maggie did not look the least bit sorry for him. Instead, excitement was shooting from her eyes. "Did you have guards?" she asked. "What were they like?"

Alexander, who had come to collect his daughter, put a restraining hand on her shoulder. "Don't badger him, darling," he said. "It is customary, if you want something, to ask politely. Remember our talks about using *please* and *thank you*?"

Maggie could feel her face and neck turning red with mortification. Of course she remembered how to be polite, but sometimes she forgot. She looked up at Grisha, intending to explain, but no words came. That happened to her sometimes when what she wanted to say was too important for any language at all.

So she placed her hand against an orange scale on his left side. For some unknown reason, orange dragon scales are the least scratchy to a human's hand. The one she put her hand over was her favorite, for it was at just the right height for her to reach. She hoped he would understand.

Grisha took her hand from his scale and held it gently between his paws. She loved how his paw pads felt like scratchy carpets worn down until smooth. She saw in his soft gold eyes that he understood all she wanted to say, and that he would never think she was rude.

"Next week," he said, "I will try to explain the Where, the When, the How Come, and the How Long."

>—•—<

All week, Grisha brooded on the best way to turn his years in the teapot into a proper dragon story. The stories the dragons told each other at the Blaue Bar were often long and boring, but at least they contained mayhem, murder, and intrigue. Poor Grisha, who had never harmed a soul, didn't see how he could tell Maggie about himself without her wishing she were listening to an entirely different sort of dragon.

Maggie clearly thought he'd been in a real prison and had fought against strife and danger. How could he tell her that the biggest threat had been the teapot breaking?

Or that his mortal enemies had been the cold and loneliness? He hated to imagine her sitting at their little table in the Blaue Bar looking bored and disinterested.

He wondered if there were a way to make his story sound exciting. He remembered Maggie saying that her father often went to the Austrian National Library, called the ONB (Österreichische Nationalbibliothek), to write his poems. The ONB, she'd said, held every story in the world, and Alexander liked to sit amongst them all as he worked. So one afternoon, after his castle was closed to visitors, Grisha took himself to the library.

Flying in the city was a matter of landing on a roof and then scaling down as close to human size as possible (usually about a foot or two taller and wider than most human adults). From there you could either fly down to the sidewalk to use the front entrance or simply look for a door on the roof. It didn't matter which way Grisha chose, as one of the great advantages of people being too busy to notice any of Vienna's dragons was that he could move about almost as if he were invisible. The D.E.E. didn't allow for free travel, but if you did your job, stayed out of the way, and didn't cause any trouble, an unscheduled trip was permitted.

Sometimes it was odd to feel so big and out of place and yet have nobody really see you. If any of the dragons strayed too long from their homes, where they were sought out and seen by tourists, they would complain of feeling like they didn't exist. Grisha, who tried to see the best in every situation, would point out that it was easier to observe people who never noticed you.

Another advantage to nobody paying him any mind was that he didn't have to ask to use the books. He simply walked through the library's stacks until he came to a very old section labeled *Europe's Long Ago and Far Away.* Right next to it were three sections on *Long Ago and Far Away* from East, South, and Southeast Asia.

Grisha looked for and read every dragon story he could find in all four sections. No matter the geographic location, almost all the stories had battles, heroes, villains, and slumbering princesses. He looked at the pile of books before him and sighed. All he'd learned was that he hated any story that began *Once upon a time.*

As he tried to think of ways to make his life sound interesting, Grisha couldn't shake off the feeling that something more terrible than being trapped in a teapot had happened. Not just to him, but to everyone who had followed a sound to Vienna. He realized that he couldn't recall why the dragons of the forest had followed the sound. Or what had happened when they arrived in the city.

Trying to remember this gave Grisha the same sick feeling he got whenever he thought of his captivity. The only clear memories Grisha had from his first few years in Vienna involved meeting Kator, Lennox, and the other dragons. Images of worried soldiers and some burning curtains flashed through his mind. But the rest seemed murky, like looking at familiar trees when the forest was thick with fog.

His bones were beginning to fill with the same chill he remembered from the emperor's palace. He told himself that he'd been reading too much and needed to go home. Once there, he'd eat some warm mash and rest. But as he walked across the large reading room, he spotted Alexander Miklós at a table near a dusty window.

Maggie's father was reading and taking notes. Sitting by his feet was a scrawny white cat with colored markings and the alert expression of a guard dog. Well, that explained the fur, Grisha thought.

It was odd how cats lurked here and there throughout Vienna. You'd see them moving about the city's grand buildings or street plazas as if they owned the land they walked on. According to the mice who lived in his dungeon, Vienna's cats felt they were too good to act as common kitchen mousers and preferred buildings that had staff in them, like hotels or museums. "That way, people bring them food," one of the mice had explained. "The cats hate catching food, but if they decide to do it, watch out!"

Grisha tried to remember if there had been cats at the Bristol, where he and Kator had originally stayed. In his mind there flashed another image from his early time in Vienna. It was of four cats with short, bushy, fox-like tails and a black dot behind each ear to distinguish them from normal cats. Grisha's teeth started to shake and the chill in his bones began to spread. In the library, the scrawny white cat, who had a regular cat's tail, merely blinked at Grisha.

Normally, Grisha would have stopped to say hello to Alexander, but the illness behind his fogged-up memories turned him away. The chill carried a persistent dread, and when he got home, he avoided the turret where he usually watched the sunset. He went straight to the dungeon and curled up like a frightened rabbit. He slept well past sunrise, and only woke up when the mice pulled on his ears, reminding him of visiting hours.

# CHAPTER TEN

# Fog of War

**When the day finally arrived that Grisha was**
due back at the Blaue Bar, Maggie woke up and realized
that she'd been thinking about him all week. Either wishing she could see him, or saving up things to tell him.
There was a new waiter at the café where she spent rainy
afternoons. Two American boys her age were staying at
the Sacher, but weren't very nice. Also, her father had
spilled espresso all across some important papers and
spent almost five minutes swearing in several different
languages.

It was odd that so much worth telling someone could
happen in only one week. It was odder still that, until now,
she'd only ever told her father her news. Which meant
that some of it never got told. After all, he already knew
about the espresso swearing. And she never told him about
kids who weren't nice to her because it upset him.

But with Grisha, it was different. The dragon had a way of seeing clearly, taking her side, and yet empathizing with everyone involved. Maggie thought of the way he'd looked at her the last time he'd been to the bar. Grisha had known she hadn't been rude, but he'd also understood why Alexander had told her not to badger him. Even before Grisha spoke, she'd felt better. When she was with him, she felt like her best self, and when she wasn't with him she looked forward to seeing him.

So this is what it feels like to miss someone, Maggie thought. Back when she'd been very little and just beginning to sort out what it meant to have a dead mother she didn't remember, she'd tried to imagine what it felt like to miss someone. Once she'd gone so far as to picture her father dying in a car crash, but that was so awful she'd had to stop right away.

Now, though, she could begin to understand without having to pretend there'd been a terrible tragedy. It would be like thinking about Grisha with the knowledge that he'd never be at the Blaue Bar ever again. That must be what missing Caroline was like for Alexander.

No wonder he looked unhappy when people mentioned her mother: It just reminded him of what he didn't have. Maggie was suddenly grateful that she didn't miss her mother. It was much easier to miss someone she knew she'd see again.

Maggie got dressed. In the sitting room where breakfast was always served, Alexander was having his first cup of coffee. He never spoke until it was finished, and Maggie normally appreciated the quiet as the day began and was usually busy with her own thoughts and plans. Today, though, she looked at her father as if seeing him for the first time. Alexander's day, no matter how busy he was, would be shaped by *not* seeing Caroline. Every day was like that for him.

Maybe he *is* used to it, she thought. Maybe he doesn't ever think about it. That was unlikely. If for some reason she could never see Grisha again, she didn't think she'd ever get used to it, and she and Grisha were only friends, not married.

Alexander put down his cup and smiled at her. "Good morning," he said. "How did you sleep? Any dreams?"

It was his usual greeting, and normally she would say, "Nothing to report," and the day would start. Grisha had said that Alexander looked like he'd fallen out of the habit of smiling and she'd replied, no, her father smiled a lot. But, as she opened her mouth to answer, she wondered what her father hid behind his eyes in those moments when he claimed he was trying to think.

"I love you, Papa," she said, and then she looked down at her roll, broke it in half, and crammed butter into it. "Nothing to report."

She added her usual response so he wouldn't suspect that it had taken her eight years to start to understand how hard her mother's death might be for him.

Alexander helped himself to what was left of the butter and said, *"Ich liebe dich ebenfalls."*

In German, the way to say "I love you too" was *Ich liebe dich auch*. But Maggie had trouble pronouncing *auch* (too) and would always use *ebenfalls* (also) instead. Normally, Alexander would make her use *auch*.

"Thanks for the *ebenfalls*," she said, and they laughed.

Their morning reset itself to normal and all was well.

>—•—<

After swearing to herself that she wouldn't fall asleep, Maggie woke up abruptly and crawled out from under the table. It was only half past one in the morning, so the dragons hadn't arrived yet. She went to the bar to order hot chocolate and fermented *Apfelsaft* from Kurt. Then she sat down at the little table where she and Grisha spent their evenings and waited, pleased that everything was ready.

When he walked in, it felt to Maggie as if the whole bar became lighter and happier. Grisha didn't like hugs because he worried about his scales scratching her, but Maggie believed in hugging people instead of only shaking hands. As a compromise, they had decided that she would put her hand on the orange scale she could reach and he would settle a front paw on her shoulder.

With that finished, he asked about her Latin progress because he knew that was her most difficult subject. Maggie told him that Latin verbs never got easier to conjugate. She described the new waiter at the café. "He's younger than all the others, but just as rude as the others," she said. "He's losing his hair, though, so maybe he's not that young."

"It's hard to tell with humans," Grisha said. "With dragons it's easy. Our scales turn silver. But sometimes humans have gray hair without being old. It's confusing."

"It *is* confusing," she said, tapping her fingers against each other and thinking that she often didn't know what to say to people she met. "People are just confusing."

Grisha had come to recognize that when Maggie tapped her fingertips like that, she was thinking about something other than what she was saying. "What's bothering you?" he asked.

"No, nothing anymore," she said, looking up from her fingers. The way Grisha's gold eyes softened into the color of lamplight when he smiled put her at ease.

"There was an American family staying at the hotel this week," she said. "A mother and three children. She travels for work and takes all of them with her wherever she goes."

"Do they have lessons the way you do?" Grisha asked.

"Yes, but not from her," Maggie said. "She hires tutors."

"Did you compare notes with them?" Grisha asked. "About what it's like to learn outside of school?"

"Not exactly," Maggie said.

She'd heard the two older boys struggling with their German translation and so had asked if they wanted help. By way of an answer, they'd told her she was stuck-up, in very bad German, and that they certainly didn't need her help.

Maggie had been too confused to respond, completely unaware that boys who were thirteen and fifteen did *not* appreciate offers of help from eleven-year-old girls. Why wouldn't you want help from someone younger? After all, when she was nine, a seven-year-old boy from Spain had shown her how to do a handstand. They'd gone up and down the Sacher's hallways on their hands until the boy saw that she could do it.

Grisha, who also had no idea why two older boys would be unkind, said, "I'm sorry that happened."

"It's just frustrating how some people are perfectly reasonable and others aren't," Maggie said. "I can never tell what it is I'm doing wrong. Or right."

"Maybe it's just a question of practice," Grisha said. "By talking to all types."

"Maybe, but I got my revenge," she said, and explained that she'd arranged for the boys' breakfast to be delivered burnt and cold during the rest of their stay. Having lived at the hotel for over seven years, Maggie had people on the staff willing to help her.

At the bar, the dragons had started in on their bragging and boasting and shouting about how *I saved him* or *I conquered an empire* or *I was conquered so that the kingdom was saved.*

"Are you going to tell me your story?" she asked.

"I'm going to try," Grisha said. "But I'm a little nervous."

"Do you want me to get my rabbit?" Maggie asked. "She helps when you're nervous."

"You have a rabbit?" Grisha asked. "I didn't think the hotel allowed pets."

"She's not exactly real," Maggie said, not feeling embarrassed the way she usually was when the subject of her rabbit came up. "I mean, I used to think so, and I carried her everywhere. And I saved her from Papa throwing her out, but now she's in my pajama drawer and I know she's . . . *stuffed*."

Maggie whispered the word, knowing it was silly but still worried about hurting the rabbit's feelings.

"I won't be so nervous that we have to disturb your rabbit," Grisha said, and Maggie nodded and leaned forward, anxious for his story.

>—•—<

Grisha need not have worried that Maggie would be bored by his lack of battle experience. She had studied the Emperor Franz Joseph's life in great detail because he had been born in Schönbrunn Palace, which was her favorite palace in all of Europe. She was thrilled beyond measure that Grisha had actually *known* Franz Joseph.

"I didn't exactly know him," Grisha said. "I just spent a lot of time in his rooms."

"And in his pockets," Maggie said, tucking her feet up under herself so that her whole body fit in the blue velvet chair. "Plus, you knew him from watching what he did."

As Grisha went on with his tale, she forgot all about the emperor and wished instead that she had lived in London with the Merdinger family. She was consumed with curiosity about Rachel and Ella, who also studied at home, but with a governess. Yakov, a banker from Budapest, seemed to be a little bit like her father, a poet from Prague; both of them spoke more than one language, cared about others, and knew of magic. I'd love to know someone whose papa was like mine, she kept thinking.

When Grisha got to the part where he and Yakov said goodbye, she said, "I wish the girls had met you. Outside of the teapot, I mean."

Grisha, who had wished exactly that for many years, smiled at Maggie. Somehow telling her about his life in a teapot had made it, if not a pleasant memory, a less painful one.

"For a while I hoped that Yakov would bring the girls to Vienna for a visit," Grisha said. "But he never came."

"What happened when you got here?" Maggie asked, but instead of answering, Grisha fell silent and his eyes took on a faraway look. Sometimes her father got lost in his thoughts when telling her stories. So she looked across the table and waited. And waited.

"Grisha?"

The dragon heard her voice and looked at her face, full of curiosity and concern. He wanted to tell her, but the usual fog that filled his mind whenever he thought of his early time in Vienna was obscuring his memories.

"I registered with the Department of Extinct Exotics," he said. After all, he must have done so. So why couldn't he remember that?

"And then?"

"They . . . had me sign a contract, and I started my job here at the castle, and, well . . . here we are."

"Was it exciting to see all of your friends again?" she asked.

"My friends," Grisha said slowly, trying to think.

"Kator and all the others," Maggie said. She noticed that Grisha looked both sad and confused. "You know, once you got to Vienna and everyone was here to register?"

"It was, um, yes, it was nice," Grisha said, although he knew it must have been terrifying. After all, he would not have worked so hard to forget what had been nice. It was odd how part of him wanted to remember, but another part warned him not to try.

"I think it's time for you to go to sleep," he said.

"I *am* tired," she said. And she was, but she also understood that Grisha no longer wanted to talk about his early time in Vienna. Still, she was curious. "Will you tell me all the rest another time?"

Grisha nodded and then went to tell Alexander that he would take Maggie upstairs and put her to bed. He'd never put anyone to bed before, but Maggie said that she didn't need much help. At the age of eleven, a kiss on the forehead was pretty much all she wanted before sleep.

"Will you come back tomorrow?" Maggie asked, as she burrowed her way under the covers.

"Next week," Grisha said. "Good night."

"It's morning," Maggie said. "Why is it always morning?"

Grisha kissed her forehead again and, instead of going back to the Blaue Bar, went home to his castle. He wrapped himself around the turret and tried to remember exactly what had happened after he'd arrived in Vienna.

Where there should be memories, there was nothing but blank space. He knew it had been wonderful to reunite with other dragons, but whatever else he'd once known remained hidden. He let the fog roll back over his memories and watched as the sun spread against the sky and bounced across the Danube as far as the eye could see.

# CHAPTER ELEVEN

# THE DEPARTMENT OF EXTINCT EXOTICS

FOR A FEW DAYS, MAGGIE WALKED AROUND IN HER own fog. It often happened that she had an idea before she had language for it. Over the years, she'd learned that searching for the right words, forcing the idea out, was about as useful as trying to make the sun move. She simply had to wait. The words would make themselves known by pressing against her mouth and head. This time, when the words finally did make themselves known, her idea was so obvious that she wondered why she hadn't known it right away.

*I want to see Grisha more than once a week.*

The dragon worked at his castle every day until three, which was just about when she stopped her studies. In theory, Maggie was free to pursue what interested her and to think her own thoughts, but in practice, her schedule was up to her father. After three or four hours of morning lessons, they had lunch. He then left her with assignments and went to the university. If and when she finished her work, she was allowed to wander the city.

If there was a thoughtful, well-reasoned argument for any deviation in Maggie's schedule, Alexander had promised he would always consider it. What she had now was not an argument, but a wish. She hoped that would be enough.

Instead of waiting for her father to look up from his desk, she stood right next to it and tapped on his arm. "I want to see Grisha more than once a week."

"Yes, that makes sense," Alexander said, as if her request had no unusual importance. He was organizing her lessons. "I'm sure we can go out to his castle one afternoon."

"No, not at the castle," she said. "Maybe he could come here after I'm done with assignments and he could . . . well, he could just be with me."

"Oh," Alexander said. He pushed his notes aside. "I should have realized. You don't want to be alone."

"No, I *like* being alone," she said. "But I like being with Grisha better."

"I suppose we could ask the D.E.E. if Grisha could be, say, your teacher, for lack of a better word."

"Grisha is my *friend*," she said. "I don't want him to be my teacher."

"I understand that," he said. "But the Department is not known for letting the dragons lead much of a life outside of their assigned jobs. And they aren't fans of such friendships."

Maggie thought about the pained expression on Grisha's face when he'd told her about registering with the D.E.E. It made sense that the Department was strict and forbidding.

"What do you say we skip lessons this morning?" Alexander asked. "We can go talk to someone there."

Normally, Maggie never got to skip lessons. Learning at home meant there was no such thing as a school holiday.

"Yes!" She ran to the hall closet and grabbed both their jackets.

"Don't get your hopes up," her father said. "The D.E.E. is very odd and full of unusual rules about what the dragons can do."

"Unusual and odd," Maggie said. "That's perfect for us."

>—•—<

Two guards armed with guns stood at the huge front entrance of the D.E.E. Their uniforms were military in style (trousers, tailored shirts, matching hats), but oddly festive in color and detail (instead of medals, their shirts and hats were festooned with large blue feathers). As Maggie and Alexander started to walk past them, the guards reached for the long swords hanging from their belts.

Without meaning to, Maggie smiled. Her love of all things military made it impossible not to be happy when seeing a sword up close instead of behind glass at a museum.

"You won't think it's funny if I run this through you," one of the guards said, his hand on the hilt, but with the blade still safely tucked in its silver case.

Maggie paused on the stairs, uncertain if she'd understood the man's German. Had he just said he would stab her?

"Excuse me, sir, what is it exactly that I heard you say to my daughter?" Alexander asked, using his most formal and elaborate German.

"You heard him," the other guard said. "Tell her to watch her expressions."

"I beg your pardon," Alexander said, moving Maggie behind him. "Are you threatening a child?"

She could hear the fury in her father's voice. He never got loud when he was mad. Instead, he was quiet and still.

"You have no business here," the first guard said, "so be off with you."

Maggie knew what was making her father mad was that he so thoroughly disliked rudeness of any kind. Personally, she felt that the blue feathers on the guards' uniforms made them look so ridiculous she couldn't imagine that the men posed any kind of real threat. The biggest danger seemed that her father would lose his temper.

"As it happens, I do have business here," Alexander said. "I need to talk to someone about a dragon."

"As it happens," the first guard said, "no one is available."

"Fine," Alexander said. "Thank you for your excessive lack of manners and help."

"But Papa, what about—" Maggie started to ask, but before the guards could react, her father simply took her by the hand and walked her briskly around the corner.

"What's the lesson here?" he asked.

"Be polite?" Maggie asked.

"Never smile at a man who is holding a weapon."

Maggie, almost running to keep up with her father, didn't feel like pointing out that she'd been smiling at the sword and *not* the guard holding it.

"We'll just look for the emperor's entrance," he said.

Maggie knew that back when Vienna had been part of an empire, most of the city's buildings were built with several entrances. There was always a secret entrance that allowed the emperor to come and go as he pleased without his subjects seeing him. It was never in the back or the front of the building, but tucked along one of the side streets.

When he'd been a young man just starting out in the world, Alexander had been a lowly clerk at the D.E.I.V. (Department of Elevator Inspection, Vienna). As a result, he had many stories about all of Vienna's regulations and decrees. Alexander had disliked the job, Maggie knew, but it had taught him a lot of useful things, like the location of the city's secret entrances. It also taught him that for every rule and contract a department had, it had an exception to that same thing.

Therefore, she was not at all surprised when her father stopped short in front of what looked like more of the building's wall. It was, on closer inspection, a door with no handle, and Alexander pushed gently against it and ushered her through.

A young, elegant-looking woman at a simple desk looked up from a book she was reading. Maggie was relieved that there were neither swords nor blue feathers in sight.

"Hello," the woman said, in English and with no trace of an accent. "She said you might figure that out."

Maggie and her father looked behind themselves, not sure if the woman was talking to them or to whom "she" referred.

"Don't be alarmed," the woman said. "I know who you are."

"Is she one of your students?" Maggie asked her father, rather doubting that she was. The woman had a cheerful look about her, while most of Alexander's students looked exhausted, worn out, and vaguely tragic. Plus this woman had excellent posture, and all of her father's students slouched.

"Goodness, no," the woman told Maggie. "It's my job to know everyone with whom the dragons have contact."

"I see," Maggie said.

"I assume you are here because of one of the dragons at the Blaue Bar," the woman said.

"We are," Alexander said.

The young woman leaned back in her chair, looking very pleased. Maggie thought it was as if she were playing a game with them, but without their knowing the rules.

"Is it the dragon who sits with your daughter?" the woman asked Alexander.

Maggie wondered how someone she'd never seen in the Blaue Bar could possibly know about her sitting with

Grisha. She felt her father's hand grip her shoulder, the way he did in crowds when he was worried about their getting separated.

"Yes, it is," Alexander said, clearly having decided to behave as if it were normal that a stranger would know where and with whom Maggie sat at night. "And I'd very much like to hire him to look after her."

"Did you know the dragons have contracts that forbid taking any outside work?"

Maggie saw something move in the distance and, for the first time, noticed that another woman was standing by a pillar several feet behind the desk, partly hidden in the shadows. That's odd, Maggie thought, and tried to make out who the woman was and what she was doing. She looked older than the woman behind the desk.

"We didn't know that," Alexander said. "But we hoped—"

"Hope has no place here," the younger woman said, and now her smile, just as bright as when they had first walked in, made Maggie angry.

"We're here for an exception," she said, hoping that her father was right and that there always was one.

The older woman laughed and moved out of the shadows. She wore a skirt and a rumpled shirt that was only partially tucked in. Her hair was pulled back in a loose bun and her spectacles were crooked. She looked brisk but tired, as if her own efficiency had worn her out.

"Well, good for you," the woman said to Maggie in German. "I'm impressed." Her eyes were so darkly blue they were almost black, but they flashed with amusement and delight.

"Does that mean you'll give us one?" Alexander asked.

"You are the first people in thirteen years to come here without wishing to file a complaint," she said. "So, yes, I think I will."

"Thank you," Maggie said.

"Go down this hall, take the staircase on your left," the woman said, "and tell them they are to do what you ask."

"Tell who?" Maggie asked.

"My assistants," she said, as if that were the most obvious thing in the world. "They'll know I sent you."

It occurred to Maggie to ask the woman who she was, but before she could get the words out, the woman said, "I am Fräulein Felinum, also called Thisbe."

"How do you do?" Alexander said politely.

"Go on now," Fräulein Felinum said. "You haven't got all day."

Maggie and her father went down the hall, turned left, and went up the stairs. They then found themselves in another hall. There wasn't a soul in sight. They wandered past some desks into a room with big windows, an oak table, several armchairs, and two napping cats. It seemed to Maggie that every important-looking building in Vienna had cats in it. But there was no one else in the room.

"Did we go the wrong way?" she asked.

"She told us to turn left," Alexander said, looking around. "But maybe she meant right?" They went back into the hall with the desks and were met by Fräulein Felinum, also called Thisbe.

"My assistants are busy and it was easy to do this myself," Thisbe said, handing Maggie a heavy, engraved envelope. "It's what you need."

Inside the envelope was a long document with several signatures and a stamp at the bottom with an affixed seal. It concerned one Benevolentia Gaudium (known informally as Grisha and legally as DR87), currently of Greifenstein Castle.

DR87, as a part-time employee of the poet Alexander Miklós, was to accompany the young Miss Miklós, currently of the Hotel Sacher, through her afternoon and evening activities. These activities were to include (but not to exceed) a meal, a walk, a story, and bedtime. Furthermore, henceforth, forthwith, and so on, all this was to take place during the hours after said castle was closed to visitors. And without a proper visa, Grisha would not be permitted to escort Miss Miklós out of the city.

"Thank you," Maggie said. "I am very glad for this."

"Now come," Thisbe said. "I will show you out."

There was no sign of the woman with good posture who'd been behind the desk when they entered. Maggie looked to the pillar and wondered whether the women took turns standing behind it.

"She's on her break," Thisbe said.

Maggie tried to come up with a reasonable way the older woman could have known what she was thinking. There really wasn't one.

"Goodbye," Alexander said. "Thank you for your help."

"Good day," Thisbe said to them. "Try not to come back. You especially, young lady."

Maggie nodded as Alexander ushered her out. Her head hurt and her skin itched everywhere. She realized that she would make every effort not to return. Thisbe had been pleasant enough, but Maggie couldn't shake the feeling that something more dangerous than strange was afoot.

# CHAPTER TWELVE

# FAVORITE THINGS

**BECAUSE THE PAPERWORK DICTATED THAT GRISHA**
be an official employee, Alexander borrowed a car and
drove out to Grisha's castle to formally offer the dragon
a job.

"Won't he think it's funny that you want to pay him?"
Maggie asked. "Or be offended?"

"I will try not to offend," Alexander said. "But I am
sure he is used to the D.F.E."

Maggie hugged her father goodbye, confident that
he would handle it all. And handle it he must have, for
the next afternoon, promptly at half past three, Grisha
arrived at the Sacher.

Maggie had had her lessons, eaten her lunch, and
finished all the tasks Alexander had left for her. She'd put
down her pencil and begun plotting out an afternoon of

walking and finding the exact right café to listen in on other people's conversations.

Just as she was deciding which streetcar to ride and in which direction, the lobby porter called. "Visitor at the front desk for you, Miss Miklós."

When she saw Grisha in the hotel lobby, Maggie realized how much she'd been wanting his company during her long, solitary afternoons. She ran toward him and skipped the last three steps.

>—•—<

Until Alexander asked Grisha to start spending his afternoons looking after Maggie, the dragon had dreaded the approach of three o'clock. The silence that would settle over the castle as the tourists left felt too much like the quiet that would fall over the shop in Budapest after it had closed and the sun had set. The fourteen hours between closing and opening held no hope of any distraction from the fact that Grisha was an unwanted teapot collecting dust.

After the castle closed to tourists, Grisha would become restless and lonely, a combination which often just felt like sadness. He'd talk to the mice who lived in a corner of the castle's dungeon, but they mostly ignored him.

Maggie was not somebody who ignored anything or anyone. She spent two weeks showing Grisha all of her favorite places in Vienna. The seven best places that sold the best almond cake. Her five favorite buildings. Her absolute favorite café for eavesdropping. Her two most favorite ways ever to walk from the Hotel Sacher to the Belvedere Palace.

"That's where Lennox lives," Grisha said.

"He's so close to the Sacher," Maggie said. "How come he's always the last one to arrive at the Blaue Bar?"

"I guess being late comes with old age."

One afternoon, as they walked behind the Parliament, Maggie pulled Grisha down one street to show him a flower box hanging from the fifth floor of an apartment building. "Isn't it pretty?" she demanded, and then, before he could answer, she was pulling him down another street so he could admire the awning of a café. "The awning and the flower box are two of my favorite things in all of Vienna," she declared.

"Everything you see is your favorite," Grisha said.

"If I make something my favorite, I won't forget it," she said. "That's how I've learned a lot of the city by heart."

Grisha, who'd heard Maggie's stories about how many times she'd gotten lost in the city, smiled. "I was just like you when I first came to Vienna," he told her. "I loved everything I saw. I tried to visit each thing I loved every day, but then I had to settle for visiting only five."

"Five is a good number," Maggie said. "But why couldn't you visit as many as you wanted?"

"Partly because the list kept growing," he said. "But mostly because the soldiers began to only let us out for two hours in the afternoon."

"I thought you were at the Bristol Hotel," Maggie said. "Not prison."

"I was," he said. "There were just strict rules about where we could go."

"Why?" Maggie asked.

Grisha thought it was a good question, but he had no answer for her. Once again he had the uneasy feeling that something dangerous was pressing up against his memories.

"How would you like to see one of *my* favorite things?" he asked Maggie, to distract her from questions he couldn't answer. "It's quite close by."

"Oh, yes, please," she said.

"It will involve a short flight," he said, lumbering down on all fours. "You can sit on my back on that patch of orange scales."

"We have to fly?" Maggie asked. "I thought you said it was close by."

"You'll see," Grisha said, and waited while she scrambled onto his back.

It was a bit tricky to fly in the city because a dragon had to go up without moving forward. It required a careful combination of moving one's wings while keeping limbs and tail very still.

Grisha unfurled his wings and he and Maggie soared up until they'd cleared the buildings, and then, with a short burst of forward motion, they had a soft landing on the roof of the Parliament.

Maggie looked very pale and wobbled a bit once she was on her own feet.

"Are you unwell?" Grisha asked.

"Just a little airsick," she said. "I was afraid I might throw up on you."

"No harm done if you do," he said.

"I've never been airsick, and I've only ever thrown up twice," Maggie said. "Both times I was angry, and it felt like being sick took the place of any shouting."

"I'm glad you're not angry," Grisha said. "But I should have realized it might not be so nice for you to be so high up."

"Oh, no, not at all," she said, craning her head back and up. "This is beyond nice."

"All of my favorite places in Vienna are rooftops," he said. "And of those rooftops, this has the best view."

They were on a slanted part of the roof, directly behind three of the marble statues that stood watch on the roof's raised edge.

"I've always loved these," Maggie said softly, staring happily at the roof's many decorations. The Parliament building had bronze chariots drawn by winged horses on each corner of the roof and countless white marble statues along its edges. She spun around happily, no longer feeling at all ill. "I never dreamed I'd see them from up here," she said.

"That was an unexpected benefit the first time I was here," Grisha said. He remembered how happy he'd been to discover this refuge in a noisy, busy, and sometimes frightening city. Grisha had guessed that because of its many statues, the Parliament roof would have shade as well as sun. He'd needed a place to think and sleep without worrying about the soldiers.

But why had he been worried about the soldiers? After all, he definitely remembered liking the soldiers, even feeling a little sorry for them.

He shook his head, which was aching beyond reason. He had a sudden and unwelcome reminder of how fear had a smell (like an electrical fire) and a taste (like vinegar). Both of which were suddenly rushing through his bones, his skin, and his heart.

The fog that normally filled the blank spaces in his memories finally rolled out, and, in its place, there were soldiers. And behind them was Leopold Lashkovic, smiling at Grisha and calling him *old friend*.

And in that moment, all of Grisha's memories came back.

His body responded as if he had been shot and he crumpled onto the ground in a ball. The sun, normally a source of comfort, felt like the stabbing of a thousand swords. Grisha spread a wing over his head, tucked his front paws up under his chin, and curled his tail around his shivering body.

His memories grew in clarity and detail. Oddly, so did his senses: He heard pigeons bickering on the roof of the nearby Palais Epstein and smelled the lunches people were eating in the Volksgarten. He heard Maggie moving toward him and felt her hand slip under his wing to rest lightly on one of his paws.

"Grisha," she said, softly. "I'm here if you need something."

He was grateful that she didn't ask any questions. "I just need to rest my head for a bit," he told her.

"I can bring you aspirin," she said, "or water."

Grisha, knowing that she could not fly off the building by herself, was surprised to find that he believed her.

If Maggie said she would do something—even find a way off the Parliament roof and then return—she would do it.

"It's not that sort of headache," he told her. "But thank you." The coolness of her hand seemed to seep through the scales of his paw and up into the burning ache behind his eyes, making it bearable.

"I hate those headaches," Maggie said. "After those boys from America were so mean to me, I had a headache that aspirin couldn't help."

"Before or after they'd tasted their breakfast?" Grisha asked.

She laughed, and the sound was everything lovely. It didn't ease any of his sorrow about what had happened to the dragons without gold eyes, but it reminded him that ugliness was not the only thing that defined the world.

Grisha pulled his wing back a bit and Maggie smiled at him. "Hello," she said. "Your colors are all pale."

"I remembered some things that I've tried to forget," he said.

"Do you want to tell me?" she asked. "You don't have to, but sometimes I feel better if I tell Papa what's bothering me. Or even my rabbit."

Grisha, picturing Maggie talking to her stuffed toy, felt his tail soften a bit. He sat up. "It's not a nice story," he told her.

"A lot of stories aren't," she said. "In the original Cinderella, the stepsisters cut off their heels and toes to try to fit into the glass slipper."

"Well, in this story no one cuts up their feet and there are no princes," he said. "But I can now answer your question about what happened when I first got to Vienna."

"Oh, yes, please," Maggie said. "Are you comfortable here? We could go back to the Sacher."

"No, I like the view from here," he said. "Dragons always want to be outdoors and somewhere high up."

"Kator told me that," Maggie said. "It's so you can see the enemy coming in battle, right?"

"That's probably how it started," Grisha said. "It seems that we've all held on to habits we no longer need."

He and Maggie looked up over the statues.

"Tell me," she said, and so he did.

# CHAPTER THIRTEEN

# GOLD EYES

**GRISHA WAS GLAD TO DISCOVER, WHILE DESCRIBING** his early days in Vienna, that certain memories still had the sparkling sunshine gleam of something new and lovely. After spending ten days in the small forest behind Yakov's house in the countryside, he had arrived in Vienna feeling new in the world. It was very similar to being a young dragon in the forest, just discovering how to scale to size, how to smell, and which parts of which trees were the best to eat. Things we all take for granted every day were, for Grisha, the most precious gifts imaginable.

Meeting Kator and Lennox as well as having a dragon community again had been marvelous in many ways. But mixed with his joy at being back in the world, Grisha could feel fear in the air. It was impossible to miss—with the hotel curtains catching fire and dragons so nervous that their tails constantly swished side to side, knocking over everything in their path. However, he'd put it down to everyone adjusting to life outside the forest.

"Kator said the sound the dragons followed to Vienna threatened them with being sent to Siberia," Maggie said. "That would make anyone afraid."

"I was so preoccupied with being free," Grisha said. "The sound should have warned me that Leopold was the man behind it all."

"Leopold Lashkovic?" Maggie asked, her voice going up shrilly. "*Your* Leopold?"

He smiled at the idea of Leopold belonging to anyone, let alone Grisha.

"How was he still alive?" Maggie asked. "People don't live to be as old as dragons!"

"They don't, that's true," Grisha said. "But Leopold stopped being a person a very long time ago. He's like a dragon in that he is a creature of magic." He paused, unsure of how to go on. He was struck once again with the difficulty of explaining magic's rules.

"Leopold gave up money to practice magic, didn't he?" Maggie asked.

She wasn't sure she understood how someone could stop being a person. Magic was obviously the reason, but it was unclear *how* it had worked to make Leopold not a person. What was he, then?

"Yes," Grisha said. "He loved money and so he never had any, just so that in return for giving it up, he could be a great practitioner."

"Time, money, or what you love," Maggie said slowly. "That seems pretty easy to follow. Why couldn't Yakov do it?"

"Not everyone has time or money," Grisha said. "And it's hard to give up what you love. Think of your father giving up poetry."

"Oh, I see," she said. For she knew Alexander would never be able to do that.

"Magic demands its exact price," Grisha said. "And sometimes that's too high."

"You must have been terrified when you saw that Leopold was in charge," she said.

"I was," Grisha said. He remembered how his fire breath had turned into a thick foam and how he had rushed out of the hotel to throw up in the gutter.

It hadn't just been the memory of being turned into a teapot that had frightened him. In setting Grisha free, Yakov had undone one of Leopold's spells, and nothing made a sorcerer angrier than that. They jealously guarded their power and would often go to great lengths to regain any power that was lost when a spell was reversed.

"But Leopold was kind to me. He said he was glad to see old friends after so many years of living alone."

Kator had been as terrified as Grisha. The four cats he'd guarded as a young dragon had been enchanted into magic by Leopold. The cats were incredibly powerful, able to change their own shapes as well as that of any living creature. They could cast spells, make potions, read thoughts, and summon lightning. The cats, Kator had said, were dangerous, but not as dangerous as Leopold.

"What do you mean 'enchanted into'?" Maggie asked.

"Somebody who isn't born into the world of magic, but becomes magical because of a spell or an enchantment," he said. "If you are *enchanted into* magic, you have been *turned into* a creature of magic."

He sounded surprised that she didn't already know that, and she was glad that he was willing to explain what was so obvious to him.

"So regular people can belong to the world of magic?" she asked.

"It's never easy, but it happens," Grisha said. "The cats were humans before Leopold turned them into cats. It's why they're so powerful. Magically speaking, that is."

"Being human and *then* a cat made them powerful?" Maggie asked. "That doesn't make sense."

What she really wanted to know was if she could have any amount of power, magically speaking, *without* becoming an animal. She knew how Leopold's magic had hurt Grisha, but the possibility that she might practice her own magic was exciting. People who know nothing about magic often think it would be exciting to practice it. That changes once they understand what magic requires of them.

"Humans almost never choose to become animals," he said. "So it's a rule that they receive more magic once they are turned into animals. An animal can also be enchanted into magic, but it won't be given as much magic as a human."

The more Maggie learned about magic's rules, the more it made sense to her that Grisha and the other dragons called it the World of Magic. It often did seem completely separate from the world in which she lived. Her world might have its own confusing rules, but at least she didn't have to worry about being turned into a teapot.

"Did you and Kator warn the others about Leopold?"

"We tried," Grisha said. "Kator told Lennox, and he told everyone not to look Leopold in the eye. He was also worried about Leopold's four cats, and so told us to avoid any and all cats."

"In Vienna?" Maggie asked. "But you were all staying in hotels!"

"Well, we knew we only had to fear the cats who had short, bushy tails and a black dot behind each ear," Grisha said. "But just to be safe, we ran every time we saw any cat at all."

"There were two cats at the D.E.E.," Maggie said. "I didn't notice their tails. I thought they were regular Viennese cats."

"They probably were," Grisha said. "Leopold's cats are somewhere in Vienna, but they don't like us."

Maggie remembered how easily she and her father had walked in and out of the room the cats were in and guessed they hadn't been Leopold's, or else they would have been attacked.

"Kator told me that once some children were throwing rocks in a field where Leopold's cats were playing tag," Grisha said. "The cats turned the kids into mice."

Maggie's mouth went very dry. Leopold's cats were definitely dangerous. "Why did he create them?" she asked. "What do they do other than eat children?"

"People paid Leopold so they could use the cats," Grisha said. He told her of the famous stories from the seventeenth century, when there'd been a long, bloody siege the cats had been hired to finish. They'd turned everyone hiding behind the kingdom's wall into wingless bugs. The attacking army had scaled the walls and then simply stepped on every bug in sight.

Maggie was silent. She wasn't sure what to do with this information. The story was disgusting as well as unbelievable. But because her friend had once been a teapot, it was probably true that the D.E.E. was run by cats who had turned people into bugs.

"Why did Leopold bring the cats to Vienna?" she asked.

"He had to call in help because he hadn't expected a hundred and fourteen dragons to arrive in the city."

"I didn't think there were more than thirty or forty of you here," Maggie said, her whole body surging with excitement. "Where are they? Can I meet them?"

"No," he told her, for this was the worst part of what had happened when the dragons arrived in Vienna. "They're gone."

Leopold had promised the soldiers he would find the dragons a peaceful role in the world. He had expected it to be easy, as he had thought there could be no more than fifty dragons left in the forest.

However, when more than a hundred dragons arrived,

the old sorcerer quickly saw that the city only had room for about forty dragons in its castles and other grand buildings. This meant that seventy-five or so dragons would need to be eliminated. At the height of his powers, Leopold could have managed such a thing, but by the end of World War II, his powers had diminished, as no one was willing to pay him for magic. He needed the cats to help him impose order on the dragons he let stay in the city as well as the ones he wanted to banish.

Deciding who could stay and who must go was tricky at first. Leopold thought about using personalities or sizes as a way to sort out the dragons. Personality, however, was hard to measure and dragons changed size depending on mood or surroundings.

And then Leopold noticed that the frail white dragon, Lennox, who seemed to be a leader of sorts, had gold eyes. Most of the others had violet eyes, and a small number of them had red.

Leopold did an exact count of whose eyes were what color, and that was that. Thirty-seven dragons with gold eyes would stay in Vienna. All the rest would have to be "processed."

"The soldiers separated dragons who'd been friends for centuries, and even dragons who were related," Grisha said.

The sound of older dragons wailing as their children were taken from them was nothing like the battle roars they all knew. The cries sounded like cellos, harps, and flutes, all horrendously out of tune.

"But Leopold was a sorcerer," Maggie said. "Couldn't he have made Vienna big enough for all of the dragons?"

"Even when he had all of his power, Leopold would only have been able to change a building's shape or purpose," Grisha said. "Not create space."

"So what did he do?" Maggie asked. "Did he send the other dragons to Siberia?"

"No," Grisha said. "If he'd had all his power, Leopold probably would have been able to turn them into paintings or plates or teapots and store them in boxes until another solution could be found."

But Leopold's limited powers only allowed for a less powerful spell. Sadly for all involved, even the cats, that spell had gone wrong.

# CHAPTER FOURTEEN

# BURIED

**MAGGIE COULD FEEL HOT LIQUID TRYING TO BURST** up from her belly, but she ignored it. She kept her hands tightly pressed together as a way of keeping what she felt, a violent mix of sad and angry, from boiling over. The idea of dragons being torn from those they loved and then falling victim to a spell worse than being turned into a teapot was beyond horrible. She couldn't believe that what Grisha described had happened in her city.

But it had happened.

After Leopold divided the dragons, the ones without gold eyes were moved to an apartment building on Weyrgasse in the third district, where they cried loudly at night. Three of them were so unhappy that they tried to escape. People who lived on the street were irritated by all of the noise and commotion.

Leopold, still unsure of where he would put the red- or violet-eyed dragons, cast a spell to keep them silent. He thought that would buy him some time while he figured out what to do with more than seventy unwanted dragons.

Instead of falling into silence, however, the dragons fell into an endless sleep, like the kind you might find in a fairy tale. It was a good spell, and one Leopold had used before, but it just wasn't the right spell for the situation. And it wasn't the spell he'd meant to use. One of the problems with having weakened power was that he couldn't always control it.

"The dragons in the apartment building still made a lot of noise, mostly from snoring," Grisha said. "Seventy dragons snoring meant a lot of smoke in the air. The neighbors complained more than ever."

Maggie tried to imagine living near an apartment building full of crying dragons. Would you really complain? Wouldn't you, instead, knock on the door and ask if they needed something? And if those dragons then fell into a deep, noisy sleep without waking up, wouldn't you call a doctor?

Maggie was sure that was what she would do.

"So Leopold moved them," Grisha said.

"Where to?" Maggie asked. Her thoughts were racing ahead, searching for ways to undo what had been done. Surely it would be a simple matter of waking up the dragons. "Where are they now?"

"I don't know," Grisha said.

It was one of the saddest parts of his memories. It was bad enough to have the dragons locked up, he thought, but not knowing where they were made it all more terrible.

"Did Leopold kill them?" Maggie whispered. Her belly roiled again.

"No, definitely not," Grisha said. "If he had, we all would have smelled it. A murdered dragon releases a horrible scent," he explained. "To get rid of the smell, the body has to be burned. It can take up to three days for the fire to go out, and then another five for the smell to vanish."

That's impressive, Maggie thought. So even a dragon who was killed on the battlefield could still cause a lot of problems for the opposing army. But what if a dragon died normally of old age? Or in a car crash?

"When we die of natural causes, we smell like pinecones or roasted acorns," Grisha said.

"Okay, so Leopold didn't kill them," Maggie said. "They have to be somewhere. Seventy-five dragons don't just vanish." Her thoughts resumed racing around one thing: Find those dragons.

"How about Siberia?" she asked. "Didn't you say that was what he was going to do if the dragons didn't follow the sound?"

"That was just a threat," Grisha said. "Leopold didn't have enough power to do that."

Right, Maggie thought. The sorcerer hadn't had enough power to turn the dragons into objects. He hadn't even been able to make them quiet without mishap.

"So where are they?"

"The rumor I heard was that he put the sleeping dragons in an old cellar somewhere. When the cats came to Vienna, they found a better, bigger place to bury them."

"Buried?" Maggie heard herself shriek. "Where?"

"We don't know," Grisha said. "Annoushka and I visited the apartment building every day, even after the spell was cast, but then the soldiers stopped allowing it."

Grisha remembered how powerless he and Annoushka had felt standing outside the building, unable to help their friends. Even worse had been the grief that flooded over them when the soldiers demanded they leave. Annoushka, the mighty warrior, had wept. The last time he'd seen a dragon cry was when his father had died. He remembered how his mother's tears had singed her face.

Maggie put her hand on his orange scale; Grisha covered her hand with the padded side of his paw. "The soldiers sent you and Annoushka away so that when they moved the dragons there would be no witnesses."

"But even if we'd been there, we couldn't have stopped them," Grisha said.

Maggie felt a tremor move through his body. It was as if she could touch his sorrow. Her own head ached as she tried to understand why nobody had helped an apartment building full of crying dragons. Dragons who suddenly began to snore instead of weep and then, just as suddenly, vanished. Had anyone even noticed?

There was something she needed to ask, some missing detail, but she couldn't pinpoint the necessary question.

"Someone has to know where all those dragons are," Maggie said.

"They're somewhere in the city, he wasn't powerful enough to move them anywhere," Grisha said. "But no one would tell us where, not even the cats."

"Wouldn't it make more sense to have asked Leopold?"

"He'd gone back to his house in Italy," Grisha said. "He left the cats in charge."

Given what she knew about the cats, Maggie wondered whether it was wise to feel relief at the news that Leopold was no longer in Vienna. But there was something else nagging her. What was it?

"How is an endless sleep different from death?" she asked. It still wasn't the missing question.

"Breathing," Grisha said. "As long as you can breathe, there's hope. There are so many stories of princes or knights who left a bleeding dragon on the battlefield, thinking he was dead, only to have to face that same dragon the next day."

Maggie's stomach twisted its knot a little tighter at the thought of dragons left bleeding on the battlefield.

"What happened to the three who tried to escape?" Maggie asked, for *that* was the question snaking through her thoughts.

"The soldiers shot them," Grisha said. "No one tried escaping after that."

That did it. Maggie ran to the roof's edge, but the throwup was faster than she was. Vomit splashed on her shoes, her dress, and the marble base of a statue as she retched up breakfast and lunch. Maggie hated throwing up for all of the usual reasons (the burning in her chest, the smell, the sound), but mostly she hated how it forced you to lean over a bucket, bowl, or bag. She'd never thrown up outside before and instead of crouching over a container, she bent miserably over the mess.

As Grisha used the smooth underside of his tail to wipe her clean, she felt the city's breeze move against her hot and damp neck. Slowly, she wiped her mouth and then leaned against the wall.

Together, she and Grisha sat in silence.

Maggie wondered how she had lived in Vienna for eleven years without knowing that seventy-seven— make that seventy-four—dragons were buried underneath. How had she loved Vienna so much—its trams, its palaces, and the cafés where you could eat almond cake—without ever realizing that something was very wrong? Was it possible that she could still love the city knowing it had turned a blind eye to so many despairing dragons?

Closing her eyes against what was unanswerable, she leaned against her friend.

"It's time to go home," Grisha told her.

Maggie stayed still, trying to picture the faces of the people who had done nothing but complain when living on the same street as a building full of scared and weeping dragons. Clearly those people, who couldn't have been *that* different from her, had forgotten what was right.

"Okay, let's go," she said, but made no move to stand up.

The key to sorting out what she'd been told was to not forget. As long as she and Grisha remembered what had happened, they would find a way to fix it.

"Are you still feeling sick?" Grisha asked, and Maggie smiled at him because she'd just thrown up, but was, in some strange way, happier than she'd ever been.

"Grisha, what would happen if you asked at the D.E.E. where the dragons are buried?"

"Nothing good," he said. "I broke one of the rules in my contract just talking about them."

"They can do that?" Maggie asked. "Tell you what to say?"

"We aren't even supposed to think about it and we definitely aren't supposed to talk about it. Not even with each other."

Maggie remembered how odd the woman at the D.E.E. had been, and how, when leaving, she'd felt as if something dangerous was hidden there. She could easily see that the Department might be the kind of place that even told your thoughts what to do.

"Is that why you forgot about what happened to the buried dragons?" she asked.

"Not exactly," he said. "I mostly forgot because it was easier than remembering. I couldn't do anything about what had happened."

"Didn't you want to try?"

Grisha thought for a minute. Had he wanted to try to confront soldiers with guns? Challenge a legendary sorcerer who would do almost anything for money? Risk the famous tempers of four cats known to be as dangerous as the sorcerer who enchanted them?

"I wanted to try to help the lost dragons in the way that I wanted to be free when I was a teapot," Grisha said.

"You felt stuck," Maggie said.

He looked at her, not sure if he could make her understand what it had felt like to be a dragon with gold eyes. You were at once profoundly lucky and overjoyed to be alive. But you were also terrified and heartbroken.

"It's like wanting something with all your heart," Maggie said. She thought of how she wanted her father to be less unhappy when he thought about her mother's car crash. "But with no idea of how to go about it."

"Yes, that's exactly what it's like," Grisha said.

That Maggie understood made him *feel* lucky. And if he, of all dragons, was lucky, then perhaps he could discover a way to make those buried dragons lucky as well. Perhaps there was a way to take them out of their sleep and restore them to life, the way Yakov had restored him.

"What if we could find them?" Maggie asked. She and Grisha knew Vienna well enough to find seventy-four buried dragons. "Couldn't we try to help them?"

"Oh, yes," Grisha said. "Yes."

Deep in his bones he wanted nothing more than to change what had happened to the other dragons. And at the same time, he wanted Maggie to be safe from the cruelty that had turned all of Vienna's dragons into unwanted and unremembered creatures. He did not try to explain any of that. He would, instead, let his actions protect her and give them both the necessary strength to do what must be done.

Maggie leaned forward to look right into the gold eyes that had saved her friend. "We will find those dragons and we will set them free," she told him.

Her words felt like a vow, and she hoped that they would be binding. She thought she understood what Leopold and the cats could do if provoked. She thought it would be worth the risk.

Grisha looked at her and touched her face very gently with the pad side of his paw. He would never let anything bad happen to her.

"I believe you," he said.

>—•—<

To free the dragons, they had to know where they were buried, and that was not the sort of information that was just going to present itself to her. For once, the library failed Maggie, no matter how many books and newspapers she checked out that mentioned anything about dragons.

There was one small paragraph in *Die Presse* about the dragons arriving in Vienna, but nothing about so many of them vanishing. She found four books on the history of dragons in Europe, one on their lives in Asia, and two that discussed language formation and its relation to a plant-based diet. There was nothing about Leopold, eye color, or the invasion of the Black Forest by trains, homes, shops, and guns.

It was as if history itself had fogged over its memories.

"Someone has to know," Maggie insisted to Grisha. They were in a café behind the Opera House, discussing what they hadn't found. "Should I speak to the cats?"

"Good lord, no!" Grisha said, and, as if to emphasize how much he meant it, fire flew out of his nose and mouth. "Excuse me," he said. "But it's a terrible idea."

"Why? *You* asked them, when Leopold went back to Italy."

"It's too dangerous," Grisha said. "Those cats are reckless and possibly crazy."

Maggie paused briefly to consider the children who'd been turned into mice by the cats and then eaten. But if the cats were truly in charge, they would know things that no one else did.

"We won't find the dragons if we avoid danger," she said. "Plus isn't the whole idea of a quest sort of crazy? Do thoughtful people go off to slay a beast?"

"No," Grisha said. "Reckless, crazy people do. Stupid people do."

"Well, we aren't stupid," she said. "We will politely ask Thisbe if we can request a meeting with Leopold's cats."

"Thisbe is not an easy human to get along with," Grisha said. "She's highly erratic, and Lennox says her judgment is not sound."

"That's what people say about Papa," Maggie said. "So she and I might get on well."

"You might," Grisha said, because anything was possible. "We'll go to the D.E.E. and find out what we can."

Normally, no dragon willingly went to the D.E.E. They had to be summoned before any of them would set a paw in the building where Leopold had once lived. But these were clearly not normal times.

Which was how Grisha knew that, at long last, he was on a quest.

# CHAPTER FIFTEEN

# FIERCE LITTLE CREATURE

As they had expected, Maggie and Grisha were stopped at the D.E.E.'s front entrance by the guards. "You need an appointment," one of them said.

"Actually, I am allowed and encouraged to visit here whenever I need," Grisha said.

"Not with a citizen," the guard answered. "Only on your own."

"*I'm* his job," Maggie said, and presented the signed, stamped document that proved it. "He can't leave me outside."

The guards conferred, as Grisha had told Maggie they would. He'd also said that it wasn't the swords or the guns she should worry about, but actually the silly feathers on their hats. They were dipped in a poison that could vaporize your insides. Maggie watched the feathers wave in the slight breeze. She'd wanted to go to the side entrance and bypass the guards altogether, but Grisha had insisted on doing everything out in the open. "I've broken a number of rules by telling you about the . . . the others," he'd said. "So I need to make sure I follow every other rule."

"Go on in, then," said the guard who seemed to be in charge of talking that day.

There was a table right by the front door, but no one was there.

"We go up these stairs," Grisha said. The stairs led to the same large hall with desks Maggie and her father had walked through. It was the hall that led into the room with the napping cats.

"We'll wait for Gregory here," Grisha said, stopping. "He is Thisbe's assistant, and we always have to speak to him first."

"Papa and I didn't," Maggie said, remembering how Thisbe had been hiding behind a pillar.

"That's because you're not dragons," Grisha told her.

They stood in the dark, drafty hall for the better part of an hour. They could hear voices in the room beyond. Finally Maggie had had enough. Shaking off Grisha's restraining paw, she headed into the room with the big windows, the oak table, the three armchairs, and the two napping cats. Only now there was just Thisbe and a young man in it. They were seated at the table, immersed in sorting through files.

Maggie stood for a minute or two, watching and expecting one of them to look up and ask what she needed. Just then something wound round her leg and she jumped a bit. It was a cat with gray and white stripes. Maggie looked closely at the cat's tail, thrilled and terrified to see that it was short and bushy. She couldn't see behind its ears to check for a black dot.

The cat hopped onto the table, making Thisbe say, somewhat sharply, "Yes, I know, but I'm busy."

Maggie made a sound that was a cross between a cough and a hiccup.

"And *you*," Thisbe said, finally looking up at Maggie. "I told you not to come back."

"I'm not here to complain," Maggie said, feeling a bit like she wanted to sit down. "I need some information."

"Do you? Well, isn't that interesting," Thisbe said, and then turning to the young man, "Gregory, take these files down to my office, will you?"

The young man—Gregory—stood up right away, putting the files in a leather satchel.

"Theodora, go get presentable and then come back straight away," Thisbe said to no one in particular, while putting papers into a drawer.

The gray-and-white cat hopped off the table and vanished through a small, low door by one of the armchairs. Maggie briefly wondered how a cat made herself presentable. Given how sharply Thisbe had spoken, it was likely that if this was one of Leopold's magic cats, they were no longer as dangerous as they had been.

Gregory strode toward the door Maggie had come through and Thisbe called out to him to please send in DR87. Then, taking a file from the desk, she sat in an armchair and motioned for Maggie to do the same. Maggie could hear voices in the hallway.

"So tell me what it is you want to know," Thisbe said.

"There are dragons buried somewhere in Vienna," Maggie blurted, just as she heard Grisha coming in.

"DR87, scale down properly and sit," Thisbe said, pointing to the third armchair.

Maggie smiled at Grisha, who was now only about a foot taller and wider than her father, and waited for Thisbe to continue. However, she simply cleaned her glasses on the sleeve of her rumpled blouse and remained silent.

"I, well, we'd like to ask where the buried dragons are," Maggie said.

Thisbe blinked. "Your friend here is in a bit of trouble," she said. "We don't pay DR87 to dwell on the past, and we certainly don't allow him or any of the DR Extinct Exotics to talk to civilians about it. Unfortunately, I can't prevent you or anyone else from being at the Blaue Bar when the DRs are droning on about their past glories. But I can certainly reprimand anyone in my charge who breaks a rule."

Maggie was surprised at how calm she felt, because she was also really angry. The fact that Thisbe or anyone at the D.E.E. thought it was okay to dictate what people or dragons could talk about was infuriating. But instead of the anger making her feel ill or shaky, Maggie saw everything in sharp detail.

The air in the room smelled of cedar and old paper. Dust scrambled in and out of the patterns the sun was making on the floor. Thisbe's darkish blue-black eyes had a golden hue.

Grisha leaned forward as if about to speak, but Thisbe cut him off. "There's no point denying anything," she said. "I have your file, DR87. For starters, you flew in the middle of the city in broad daylight."

"That's not against the rules," Grisha said, but Maggie heard the fear in his voice.

"Excuse me," Maggie said, looking at Thisbe and speaking in a loud, clear voice. "His name is Benevolentia Gaudium or Grisha. It is not DR87. And, yes, he did fly, but let me remind you that it isn't forbidden as long as he doesn't leave the city. And if any tourists had seen him fly, they'd have been thrilled."

"I see I will need a file on *you*, Anna Marguerite Miklós," Thisbe said. "Right now, all I have is that you are a half-orphaned girl child of eleven years and a resident at the Hotel Sacher."

Half-orphaned? Girl child? Maggie wasn't sure if she should be alarmed or just laugh.

Before she could make up her mind, a young woman walked into the room, followed by Gregory, who was carrying a tray with a pitcher of water and two glasses. It was the woman Maggie and Alexander had met on their first visit. The one with good posture.

The woman chose a stool next to Thisbe's chair. She sat very still, radiating a graceful boredom.

Gregory handed the woman a glass of water. Maggie watched with fascination as the woman peered into the glass and lapped at the water with her tongue. Then she stopped abruptly and looked up with an expression of displeasure.

"It's too cold," she said, and handed the glass back to Gregory.

Everything about the way she moved reminded Maggie of a ballerina. Even the woman's hands were graceful and elegant.

"This is Theodora," Thisbe said. "She's not terribly fond of humans."

"Why are you here?" Theodora asked. "I thought Thisbe told you not to come back."

"I'm here for information," Maggie said. "Either you will give it to me or you won't. But as you have already kept us waiting for over an hour, I would appreciate getting an answer now."

"Maggie, *don't*," Grisha said, his voice low. "Please."

"Fierce little creature," Theodora said, and then, to Thisbe, "What information?"

"To know where the dragons are buried," Maggie snapped, cutting off Thisbe.

"There are no buried dragons," Theodora said. "It's all a rumor."

"Thisbe has already admitted that there are," Maggie said.

"Actually, what I said was that DR87 had broken a rule by speaking to you about them."

"Grisha broke a rule by telling me about buried dragons that don't exist?"

"Yes," said Theodora and Thisbe at the same time.

"If you are going to lie to me," Maggie said, "then please go to the trouble of making it believable."

"Maggie, you cannot talk to them like that," Grisha cried out, and at the same time, Gregory said, "I'm sure Miss Miklós didn't mean to sound disrespectful."

"Gregory, you may take your leave," Thisbe said, her dark eyes fixed on Maggie. "Theodora and I will deal with this . . . girl child."

Gregory hurried to the door, clearly delighted to be leaving.

"She's new to magic. She didn't know," Grisha said. "Forgive her."

"DR87, do hush," Thisbe said, and Theodora giggled. "You too," she snapped, and then placed her hand on

Theodora's head, saying, in what Maggie recognized as Latin, "*Without memory may your soul sleep.*"

Immediately the young woman stretched and yawned, and as her long, thin body curled onto the stool, it changed seamlessly into that of a napping cat. A gray-and-white-striped cat with a short, bushy tail. No doubt she also had a black dot behind each ear.

The change from austerely graceful woman to curled, sleeping cat was beautiful and terrifying all at once. Maggie stared, frozen in place. It was one thing for Grisha to talk about magic and science, the odd and the unusual. It was quite another to see it happening before her eyes. And it was slowly dawning on her that Thisbe was no ordinary person.

"We don't have a lot of time," Thisbe said. "This doesn't last for long."

"We'll leave now," Grisha said, standing up, but staying the size Thisbe had demanded of him. "We won't come back. You don't have to demonstrate anything further."

Maggie saw that his tail, usually so still and strong, was shaking.

"Calm yourself, DR87," Thisbe said. While she spoke, she wrote on a pad next to the water tray Gregory had abandoned and held it up to them.

*Leopold has spies everywhere, but especially in this building.*

"I'll show you out," she said.

Maggie felt dizzy when she stood to follow Grisha and Thisbe. It was as if every thought she'd ever had was reorganizing itself. People and cats were one and the same. Latin was actually useful. A rumpled woman with glasses and messy hair had magic power. Her head ached. As they left through the side entrance, Maggie was relieved that the city looked unchanged.

"I'm sorry for what I'm about to do," Thisbe said. "But it's important that Miss Miklós understands the consequences of not obeying me."

"Oh, no," Grisha said. "Please don't—"

He never finished, for as soon as Thisbe whispered, "*Vacate et collapse,*" Grisha froze and then shrank down so dramatically that he fell to the ground. He lay on the sidewalk, the size of a marble, vaguely green, and horribly still.

"No," Maggie screamed. "No!" Her breath was full of ragged gulping, but she was entirely too terrified to cry.

"Do be quiet," Thisbe said. "The guards have no idea about this entrance. I don't want them to hear you and come rushing round." She picked up Grisha and handed him to Maggie.

"You haven't killed him," Maggie said, her breath still ragged but quieting down. She could feel the small but steady breath moving through the tiny-sized Grisha in her hands. "Thank you."

"Don't thank me. If you put Theodora or me in danger, I will destroy everything you care about," Thisbe said. "Do you understand?"

Maggie nodded. She didn't just understand it; she knew the woman wearing smudged glasses and a frumpy tweed skirt was capable of making good on any threat.

"I, I, I—"

"Be quiet," Thisbe said, which was unnecessary, as Maggie had stuttered into silence. She wanted to say *I am a harmless human and you are one of Leopold's cats.* But she was incapable of speech.

"Don't go to the library again," Thisbe said. "Looking for information about the buried dragons has alerted Leopold. I will send him a report saying you have stopped searching."

"We won't ever look for the buried dragons," Maggie said, wishing her voice sounded less weak and wobbly. "I promise."

Thisbe hadn't killed Grisha, but she had demonstrated that she could and would if she had to.

"You can't give up," Thisbe said. She looked indignant and disapproving. "You and Grisha are the only hope those poor beasts have."

"I thought you just told me to stop," Maggie said, still terrified and exhausted, but now also confused and with eyelids that were dangerously hot and scratchy with tears.

"I'm trying to help you look without you risking Leopold finding out what you're doing," Thisbe said. "Do you understand?"

"Wait—you want to help us?" Maggie was trying to remain calm, but kept looking down at Grisha to make sure he was alive.

"I forget that humans are such annoyingly emotional, fragile things," Thisbe said. "Pay attention."

While she had none of Theodora's exaggerated grace, Thisbe had a ferocious intensity that was scary but fascinating.

"You must do exactly as I tell you," she continued. "First, find a potion to reverse the spell Leopold used on the dragons. Only then can you worry about where they are."

"Where do I find a potion?"

As soon as the words were out of her mouth, Maggie regretted them. Thisbe's dark eyes looked as if a black flame was sparking inside them.

"Clearly, if I could tell you that, I wouldn't tell you to find one, would I?"

"Right, sorry," Maggie said. She felt dizzy. If once she'd thought she was afraid of spiders or of the dark, she now understood that fear was what you felt when someone you loved was in danger.

"When you have the potion, you will ask Kator to help you find Tyr," Thisbe said. "She can tell you where the dragons are."

"Who's Tyr?" Maggie asked. "I don't understand."

"You don't have to understand that yet," Thisbe said. "Just repeat back what I said."

Maggie stared at her dumbly before stuttering out, "Wh-which part?"

"Oh, for heaven's sake," Thisbe said, taking hold of Maggie's chin between her thumb and forefinger. She looked right past Maggie's brown eyes into the center of her mind. Maggie could feel her in there. It was, Maggie thought, like having the worst sort of headache, accompanied by painfully itchy skin.

"What a mess you are in here," Thisbe said. "I should have expected as much. Humans get so upset when they first see the world of magic."

Maggie wanted to explain that seeing a woman turn into a cat and then a friend being reduced to the size of a marble would upset anyone. But all she could do was nod. *Yes, I am a mess.*

"Now pull it together."

Maggie nodded again.

"First, find a potion to reverse what Leopold used to make the dragons sleep. Then ask Kator to help find Tyr. Repeat that."

Maggie did.

Thisbe let go of her chin and the thumping in Maggie's head stopped.

"I once tried what you're attempting," Thisbe said, a small hint of softness coming into her face. "It's more dangerous than you know." She pushed the side door open and started to go back in the building.

"Wait! Please!" Maggie cried. "Please put Grisha back to normal."

"Oh, for heaven's sake," Thisbe repeated and, waving a hand, said, *"Et reverse repair."*

Maggie looked intently at Grisha, who remained small but was clearly growing. When his size became bigger than her hand, she put him on the ground, intent on watching as he grew.

But Thisbe placed a finger back under Maggie's chin and looked her in the eyes. "I had a friend once and Leopold took her," Thisbe said. "Guard your friend."

# CHAPTER SIXTEEN

# LEOPOLD'S CATS

**EVEN WITHOUT MAGGIE SAYING ANYTHING, GRISHA** guessed what had happened. His joints and bones ached. Scaling up and down is a natural part of a dragon's life, but the extremes Grisha had undergone in such a short time caused pain and discomfort. While he'd been a size no dragon willingly became, he'd had all the usual fears that any victim of enchantment does, but he'd been comforted by knowing that Maggie was safe. Her voice and Thisbe's had been roars of thunder to his tiny ears. It had been impossible to make out any words, and so he waited patiently, leaning against the wall, while Maggie told him what Thisbe had said.

"She seemed scary, but also scared," Maggie said. "I just couldn't tell if she was trying to help or sending us on a pointless chase."

"Maybe both," Grisha said.

"Who's Tyr?" Maggie asked, and Grisha was glad that her voice had stopped shaking.

"She was one of the four women Leopold enchanted into cat form," Grisha said. "But I thought she'd died. There used to be four of them. One died, and one's missing."

Once he'd known all of their names: Thisbe, Tyr, Theodora . . . and? Well, whatever her name, she and Tyr were the two who were no longer around.

"Where would we get a potion?" Maggie asked. "Thisbe said not to go to the library or Leopold would know we were searching, so looking it up in a book is out."

"We wouldn't find it in a book," Grisha said, remembering once more how little his human friend knew about magic. "One of the reasons that the world of magic has largely disappeared is that no one wrote anything down. Most of the forest creatures can't read, and humans taught each other secretly without leaving a record."

"But Thisbe told us not to give up," Maggie said, feeling defeated. "What do we do?"

"First," Grisha said, "we walk home very slowly."

Maggie put her hand on the orange scale and they made their way back to the hotel, both longing for a hot meal and a long nap. Fortunately, those were two things the Sacher could easily provide.

>-•-<

In the early morning before dawn, Grisha had the unwelcome surprise of waking up to find a cat staring at him. It was a mostly black cat whose white throat and white paws gleamed brightly against the dark.

"I'm not so fond of cats," Grisha said. "Would you mind changing shape?"

"I didn't bring clothes," Thisbe said. "Next time."

"That's okay," Grisha said, fervently hoping that there wouldn't be a next time.

"I'm afraid I alarmed that girl child of yours," Thisbe said. "I haven't been a human in so long that I have almost no memory of how confusing magic can seem."

"You shrank me down to pea size," Grisha said. "Of course she was alarmed."

"I've waited a long time for a DR to try to free my unfortunate friends," Thisbe said, her short, bushy tail swishing back and forth. "I never dreamed it would be you, DR87."

"*You* have the power needed to free them," Grisha said. "Why don't you do it?"

"We tried it once," Thisbe said.

"What happened?" Grisha asked. He very much doubted that Leopold's cats had tried to help the buried dragons.

"It's a long story."

"I'm not going anywhere," Grisha said, although part of him wished he could. He didn't think Thisbe had come to harm him, and, after all, she'd been worried about spies at the D.E.E. However, it was impossible to shake off his fear of Leopold's cats. They didn't just report back to their boss in Italy: They had their own gruesome reputation. Even without remembering the past, the lingering ache in Grisha's bones reminded him of what Thisbe could do.

The cat arched her neck and back before settling onto the floor, her white-tipped front paws neatly tucked in front of her. Grisha, who was sitting in the exact same way, curled his tail around himself for warmth and comfort.

"When we first came to Vienna, Leopold had already been at work sorting out you lot," Thisbe said. "We thought he would have us do the things he'd become too weak to do: errands, odd bits of magic, that sort of thing."

"Do you know what had made him so weak?" Grisha asked.

There had been a rumor that the spell had caused a great number of the sleeping dragons to fall ill. If the rumor were true, it would mean their friends were in pain.

It seemed impossible that Leopold would have done such a thing on purpose: Illness would cause the noise of sick dragons, but also the terrible stench if his spell killed them. How could a man whose fame had been unparalleled botch a spell so badly? No one knew of a rival sorcerer who might have undone enough of Leopold's spells to make his powers so erratic.

"During the last war, a bomb destroyed a warehouse full of objects," Thisbe said. "Precious objects Leopold had enchanted. Naturally, once his creations vanished from existence, Leopold became significantly weaker in both body and soul."

So that was it. No rival sorcerer; just a weapon from the world of men.

"And so he summoned the four of you," Grisha said, surprised to find himself feeling a bit sorry for Leopold. Imagine watching much of your life's work burst into flames.

"Yes, and we came to Vienna happily, because his villa near Rome is very damp," Thisbe said. "We didn't know our job would be to keep dragons prisoners, both above and below ground." She reached a paw over Grisha's tail and tapped gently on his front paws. "I know you are better off than those who are buried, but your life is horribly regulated. If it were up to me, you all could wander freely. But it is not so."

For the first time Grisha realized that while the dragons needed Thisbe's permission in order to do anything, Thisbe needed Leopold's.

"Tyr said we were obliged to remember what life was like before Leopold enchanted us into magic. Most of us had been orphans, and all of us were very poor."

"I didn't know that," he said. "Rumor was that you'd all been evil witches."

"Rumors are usually wrong," Thisbe said drily. "Tyr and I were kitchen maids trying to teach ourselves to read when Leopold offered us power beyond our imaginations."

"He gave you a choice?" Grisha was surprised. He knew that most humans were enchanted without agreeing to it. If you weren't born into the world of magic, it could be a terrifying place.

"We were poor and desperate for a better life. Tyr was the one who made sure never to forget our life before magic," Thisbe said. "So after the war, after he summoned us for help, after Leopold had cast his spell, she insisted that we risk everything to free others as we had once been freed."

"By using magic," Grisha said. "Didn't you guess Leopold would sense it and stop you?"

Because the cats were Leopold's creations, their magic was connected to his, so when they used it, he would know.

"Leopold was so much weaker than ever before that we believed we could prevent him from finding out."

"He's the one who enchanted you," Grisha said. "His magic is forever connected to yours."

"Tyr thought we had a clever enough plan to keep him from knowing," Thisbe said. She fell silent for so long that Grisha wasn't sure if she would continue.

"Tyr and I were each going to give up our magic in exchange for a two-part spell that would wake the dragons and make the sick ones healthy," Thisbe said. She spoke slowly, as if the words cost her a great effort. "Tatiana was going to give hers up for a spell to prevent Leopold from finding us out. Magic for magic, all around."

Tatiana! That was the fourth cat. Grisha knew he'd known her name.

"Tyr said Theodora should hold on to her magic so that when we went out into the world, it could protect us. It had been a very long time since we'd lived without magic's protection, and we all remembered how awful that was."

Grisha knew that magic didn't make life safe, but if you had lived with it for a long time, magic was familiar and comforting.

"Our plan would have worked beautifully but for one mistake," Thisbe said. "Tatiana went into Leopold's room, and Tyr went to where the dragons were being held."

That's not a mistake, Grisha thought. Spells worked better when cast close to their target. It's why Leopold had come into the forest to find a creature.

"I stayed behind with Theodora," Thisbe said. "The plan was that we would wait for Tatiana to return, and then all go join Tyr and the dragons, so I could do my part of the spell to wake the dragons. Then Theodora would take us all to Rome, where we'd blend in and learn to be normal cats."

Grisha was hard-pressed to see how there was a mistake. It seemed like a good plan.

"We hadn't coordinated our timing," Thisbe said, "and by chance, Tyr and Tatiana gave up their magic at the same time."

"Oh," Grisha said softly. The simultaneous double action would have alerted Leopold to their magic before Tatiana's spell had had a chance to take hold.

"He was so angry that he didn't think, and he broke Tatiana's neck," Thisbe said, her voice both angry and sad. "She had been keeping watch in his room."

Grisha was horrified and amazed. Horrified that Tatiana had died in such violence and amazed that Leopold had been so careless in his rage. In murdering one of his cats, he'd reversed one of his own major spells and lost yet more precious power.

"Killing her made him even weaker, of course," Thisbe said. "He didn't have enough power left to stop Tyr on his own, so he sent his guards after her. I knew the moment they caught her."

Grisha had seen what the guards could do and could well imagine what they'd done to a cat who'd disobeyed Leopold *and* given away all her power for a spell.

"The minute her life was at stake, I abandoned our plan. Instead of doing my part of the spell to wake the dragons, I used my magic to erase the guards' memories and they let her go."

Grisha was reminded of the cats' reputation for ruthlessness. Even, as in this case, in the face of real danger, to erase someone's memories was a form of murder.

To make yourself forget something, as he had done about his early time in Vienna, was cowardice, or, if you were feeling kind, a sort of self-protection. But to do it to someone else could only be seen as murder. What we remember makes us who we are.

Grisha knew that remembering the forest's lessons about staying alive had shown him how to do so while trapped in a teapot. Without his memories, he knew, he might as well be dead.

"Leopold was so enraged that I'd saved Tyr that he erased Theodora's memories. He knew that would punish me even more than killing her," Thisbe said. "She has no idea that he killed Tatiana. She doesn't even remember her, or Tyr. She was such a brilliant, fun creature before Leopold destroyed her mind."

Grisha thought of the graceful young woman he and Maggie had met. He might have called her elegant or even pretty, but certainly not brilliant or fun. Grisha felt terribly sorry for Theodora, who was walking around in a half-dead state with no memory of who she'd once been. He was also angry at all the destruction Leopold had caused with no harm befalling him.

"Leopold must have been very weak after he stole her memories," Grisha said. "It's astonishing that he took the risk."

"He was just weak enough for me to cast a spell so that he could never harm Tyr."

"What did you give up?" Grisha asked, although he could guess.

There was only the slightest of pauses before the cat answered. "Ever seeing Tyr again."

There was no anger or sadness in Thisbe's voice. Just the matter-of-fact tone of someone who knew the rules. Not for the first time, Grisha thought of how cruel magic could be.

"Tyr can tell you where the dragons are."

So could you, Grisha thought. Why don't you?

"Benevolentia Gaudium, you have no reason to trust me," Thisbe said. "But to answer your unasked question, I can't tell you where the dragons are because in order to protect *my* memories from Leopold, I gave up trying to free the beasts."

Grisha curled and uncurled his neck. "But you are here at my castle," he said. "Behaving as if you want to help."

"I can relay facts," Thisbe said. "One can't argue with facts. But I can't help directly." Grisha not only heard the regret in Thisbe's voice, he could see it in the intense darkness of her eyes. "You need a potion to finish what we tried to do."

"You make it sound like finding a potion is easy," Grisha said.

"No, I make it sound like it's what you must do," Thisbe said. "I am alone on the D.E.E. roof until four or five most mornings, should you need me."

And then she vanished. Grisha did not think that was an act of magic so much, but rather the normal behavior of a cat. Who were, after all, odd and disturbing creatures even when they were not enchanted.

# CHAPTER SEVENTEEN

# PERMISSIONS

**MAGGIE THOUGHT THAT SINCE SHE AND GRISHA** couldn't go to the library, there was only one other thing that might lead them to find a potion.

"Let's get cookies," she said. "That always helps."

They went down to the Sacher's small and very red lobby. It was where Maggie had always done her most important thinking or game playing on rainy days. Finding a potion was going to require some combination of thinking and make-believe. But first she ordered two grenadine and sodas and eleven cookies neatly laid out on a gold-and-white plate.

Grisha looked suspiciously at the bright red liquid in his glass. "It's really good," she told him. "Plus, it smells a lot better than fermented *Apfelsaft*." She was delighted when, after a cautious sip, he downed the whole glass in one gulp.

Maggie looked around the lobby. There was the usual sight of men and women dressed in business attire, collapsed into the lobby's inviting chairs and reading the paper. More casually dressed people were enjoying afternoon coffee and cake. She loved the idea of plotting out a magical plan while surrounded by so many unsuspecting grown-ups.

"Let's review what we know about how to reverse a sleeping potion," she said.

"I know nothing at all," Grisha said.

"Me neither," Maggie said. "Not even Papa knows about reversing sleeping potions. I asked at breakfast."

"The only person I ever met with a potion was Yakov," Grisha said.

"That's it," Maggie said, sitting up straight and almost knocking over her empty glass.

"What's it?"

"Let's go to London and ask him," she said. "Wouldn't the potion that got you out of the teapot wake up buried dragons?"

"Maggie, Yakov was almost sixty-five when I left London," Grisha said. It had been forty years since World

War II had ended. Maggie did the math and accepted that Yakov probably hadn't lived to be a hundred and five. But still the possibility existed that the same potion Yakov had used to free Grisha might also rouse dragons from a terrible, buried sleep.

Could she and Grisha find it? Yakov might be dead, but surely not everyone in the Merdinger family would be.

"Do you think the girls might still be in London?" Maggie asked.

"Rachel and Ella?" Grisha asked. "Well, yes, they might be. Much older, of course."

"Don't you think that Yakov would have left them his potion, you know, in his will?"

"I suppose," Grisha said. Just thinking about Yakov's daughters made him happy. He much preferred being able to smell, see, and feel the sun for himself, but he remembered when Rachel and Ella had brought the outdoors inside with them. In London, the girls were the sun.

"Will you be able to find where Yakov used to live?"

"London is a very big city," Grisha said. "And they've probably moved. It might take me a day or so to track down their smell."

"Then we can go?"

"Well, it's the only idea we have," Grisha said. "And it would be splendid to see the girls again. So, yes, we can go."

Maggie promptly asked a waiter for another plate of cookies and Grisha looked at her quizzically. "It's to celebrate," she said. "I've only ever been to London with Papa and that was not so much fun." It hadn't been terrible, but there had been a very large number of art and history lessons involved. Travel, Alexander was fond of saying, is the world's best classroom.

>—•—<

But apparently travel to London *without* her father was not the world's best anything. "No, absolutely not," he said. Maggie patiently listened to the reasons Alexander gave. It was dangerous and a fool's errand besides. "You'll miss lessons for no reason," he said. "Plus you are only eleven. That's too young to travel abroad without me."

Normally Maggie would embark on a long campaign of wearing him down. After all, that was how she had finally been allowed to go to the Blaue Bar at night, which was how she had met Grisha, which was the best thing ever. But she didn't have time for such a campaign. The sleeping dragons depended on her going to London. She'd have to think quickly of a way to secure her father's permission.

How did you turn a quest into a thoughtful, well-reasoned argument to skip lessons and fly to another country? Especially when it involved asking two strangers for a potion they might not even have. It was true, as Grisha pointed out, that the dragons weren't going anywhere. But Maggie felt strongly that such an important quest should not be interrupted because of an unreasonable parent.

"He's not being unreasonable," Grisha said. "And we have a more serious problem. I will need a visa."

"Do we have to go back to the D.E.E. to get it?" Maggie asked.

"I can go alone," Grisha told her. "I know how to find her."

He tried explaining how Thisbe was only alone in the early hours of the morning, but that made Maggie even more determined.

"I'm coming with you," she said. "It's not like Papa doesn't let me stay up late anyway."

Grisha waited up with Maggie until past one in the morning and then flew her across the city's low, murky sky. They landed quietly on the roof of the D.E.E. and at first saw no one. Then, in the shadows, they spotted a small creature moving confidently atop the building's edge.

"She's there," Maggie whispered, as the cat, its back to them, sat suddenly still.

Grisha, who did not believe in sneaking up on enchanted cats, coughed gently, and the black cat with white throat and paws turned. It tilted its head slightly before stretching and curling into a woman dressed in rumpled clothes and wearing spectacles. Her hair was in a ponytail instead of its usual bun.

"Hello," Thisbe said, once she was no longer in cat form.

Grisha, thinking back to her visit to his castle, said, "I thought you had to have your clothes with you to make the transition from cat to a dressed human."

"Of course not," Thisbe said. "I'm enchanted. I can do as I please."

"So you lied," he said, feeling a bit aggrieved.

"Normally I prefer my cat form," Thisbe said. "However, if the child intends to challenge Leopold, she needs to get used to the world of magic."

Grisha looked over at Maggie and was glad that she looked far less astonished than when Theodora had changed shape.

"We need a visa," Maggie said, and, before Grisha could stop her, she explained all about Yakov and his potions.

"I did not know this part of your history, Benevolentia Gaudium," Thisbe said. "If you find the girls, I hope it will work."

"Does that mean you'll give Grisha a visa?" Maggie asked.

"Oh, he doesn't need anything," Thisbe said, waving a hand. "I say a visa is needed because I have to be certain no dragon leaves the city without my knowing it."

"Why can't they just go when and where they want?" Maggie asked. She was beginning to understand her father's irritation with rules that made no sense.

"Because they'd be violating the spell Leopold cast to keep them in Vienna. He'd be alerted, the guards would go after the dragon, and I'd have a murder on my hands. Not pleasant for anyone."

"So it's for safety," Maggie said.

All of Vienna's dragons are connected to Leopold through the spell that had brought them out of the forest, Grisha thought. The sorcerer's magic had kept them all in the city, above or below ground.

It struck him that he himself had never heard the sound that all the others had. He had come to Vienna willingly and stayed because of the soldiers with guns, but also because he craved the company of other dragons.

His head suddenly ached and all of the scales on his paws and tail began to itch. Thisbe was inside his mind.

"And you had nowhere else to go," Thisbe said. "That's mostly what kept you here."

"Please don't do that," he said. "It's rude."

Thisbe laughed, but Maggie looked alarmed. "Grisha," she said. "Don't make her mad."

"I'm not mad," Thisbe said. "I just have the bad habit of walking into the thoughts of other creatures. It was the first power Leopold gave us. Tyr and I spent the whole day listening in on thoughts. We found out that all of Prince Einar's horses had colic. His groundskeeper was stealing money by feeding the horses contaminated feed."

"What happened to them?" Maggie asked. She loved horses and could almost picture Tyr and Thisbe, still maids in a castle, trying out their new power and stumbling onto a crime.

"Tyr told the prince that if he didn't hire a new groundskeeper and buy some medicine for the horses, she would tell the king."

"How could she possibly get to tell a king?" Maggie asked. She had very little idea about how a castle worked. A kitchen maid could change the course of a kingdom, especially if she knew how to read and write.

"Oh, put a note on his father's bed or dinner tray or something. Quite simple," Thisbe said. "Tyr was so clever that way. She could listen in on thoughts without causing the headache."

"Or itching?" Grisha asked.

"Can't avoid that," Thisbe said. "Itching is the body's natural response to another being walking into your mind and reading your thoughts."

"I don't even need *anyone's* permission to leave the city, do I?" Grisha asked. "The magic Leopold used to bring the dragons to Vienna didn't bring me here. He and I haven't been connected by magic since I escaped the teapot, which reversed the spell that connected us in the first place."

"Correct," Thisbe said. "But to make sure, I will give up a memory and cast a spell of protection to keep Leopold from detecting what you are doing."

Grisha, aware of how precious his own memories were, hesitated.

"I appreciate your concern, Benevolentia Gaudium, but I do it willingly," Thisbe said, clearly knowing his thoughts, explaining why his tail still itched. "If it makes you feel better, I will use the memory of the day Tyr and I first used our power to listen."

"The one you just told us about?" Maggie asked, and Thisbe nodded.

"We will take such good care of it," Maggie said. "I will never forget it."

Grisha, in that moment, did not think he had ever loved anyone more.

>—•—<

Maggie's impatience to get to London grew along with her well-thought-out reasons for going. She was only willing to wait until lunch the next day before trying to change her father's decision. Alexander ate the same meal each afternoon: grilled fish with green salad, a bottle of mineral water, and an espresso.

She waited until he'd taken his first sip of espresso and began. "Papa, I've given a lot of thought to why you think I shouldn't go to London. And I was wondering if we could discuss it further." Her father often said how important it was to discuss any disagreements.

"Of course we can," Alexander answered. "I'm always delighted to hear your thoughts."

"Well, Grisha will be with me, so it's unlikely to be dangerous," she said. "After all, if you didn't trust him to protect me in a city, you would never have hired him."

"I certainly trust him," Alexander said. "But Vienna is a city you both know already."

"You only trust him because we know the city?" she asked. "I wish we hadn't walked so often in neighborhoods we'd never seen before. I didn't know that I was only protected in our neighborhood."

Alexander put down his cup and looked at his daughter. "That *is* a lot of thought," he said dryly. "But listen, Maggie: You are only eleven years old. I will take you to London in the fall and we can go to the theater and the

British Museum and have a great time. But I cannot let you and Grisha wander through London on some wild goose chase for a magical spell."

"Potion," Maggie said. "And—"

"Potion," Alexander said, "but you cannot gallop around London—"

"On a fool's errand, yes, I know. You said that yesterday," Maggie reminded him.

"I was going to say on a whim, but fool's errand will do just as well," he said.

"That's what I've thought of the most," Maggie said. "I'm a poet's daughter—you always say that's why I have an education based on freedom and responsibility and being creative and all that, right?"

"I do say that," Alexander said, slowly. "And?"

"What sort of errand should I be going on, if not a fool's? Did you hire Grisha so I could go on sensible ones?"

"Oh, God," he said quietly. "I'm beat."

"And as for being eleven, well, that's true, and soon I will be twelve, and then fifteen and then—"

"Learn to quit while you're ahead, Mags, my dear," her father said, standing up. He had never called her Mags before, and she rather liked the sound of it. It reminded her of a short, fashionable haircut in a way that the name Maggie, which fit her long and ordinary hair, never could.

"If it weren't the middle of the day, I'd need a drink," he said. "You can go to London."

"Oh, thank you!" she said, both deeply pleased and a bit surprised. It was the very first time she'd ever triumphed in a disagreement with him.

# CHAPTER EIGHTEEN

# Yakov's Daughters

AS THEY FLEW OVER THE COUNTRIES BETWEEN Austria and England, Maggie grew warmer and warmer in spite of all the air rushing past them. She was glad for a chance to cool off when Grisha splashed down into the Thames. It was a very good river in which to land, as it ran through London in much the same way the Danube ran through Vienna. He placed her carefully on the riverbank and then swam a bit to get his temperature down.

Maggie was surprised that none of the hundreds of people she could see had paid any attention to their landing. It was true that in Vienna, people rarely noticed Grisha. But it was one thing to witness people not paying attention, and quite another to find that no one sees you when you fly in on a dragon.

"Once factories, railroads, and streetlamps were built, the world sped up," Grisha said, hoping to explain. "After that, no one had enough time to see us."

"Doesn't it feel strange?" she asked.

"Sometimes it does," he said. "Kator hates being ignored, but I find it somewhat useful."

"I know this many people are not blind," Maggie said, pointing to everyone in London rushing here and there. "How can they not see you?"

"They don't want to," Grisha said. "We don't really belong in the world of men, and no one likes to waste time on things that don't belong."

Every bit of Maggie bristled to think the dragons felt they didn't belong. But she had to consider that perhaps it was as simple as dragons being too slow for a fast world. It did take a lot of time to notice Grisha; of course it did. He moved slowly, changed his size, had a voice filled with music, and the smell of fire hovered about him. He was the most unusual person Maggie had ever met.

After his scales had cooled sufficiently, Grisha put her on his back again and clambered up into the streets of the city. Maggie slid off onto firm ground and Grisha stuck out his tongue to inhale deeply. She loved watching him when he was at his most dragonlike, and smelling the world was one of those times.

Grisha and Maggie went left and then right and then straight, depending on the smells he recognized. Some smells were very familiar to Grisha and some of them were shockingly new. London was certainly very different from when he'd last lived there, but like all cities, it kept its essential qualities—the things that made it London instead of, say, Paris or New York.

He kept following the familiar smells, and soon they arrived outside the building where Yakov and his family had lived. It was just off Eaton Square and once had been a pleasant, although not overly fancy, place to live. Now, however, it was a small neighborhood in which only the very richest people had homes.

Grisha took a breath into his mouth and could smell the scents of lonely children, leather bags, champagne, fresh flowers, stewed tea, and sadness. "The girls aren't here," he said. "There's no trace of them." Grisha sounded as sad as bagpipes at a funeral.

"I thought you'd be able to smell them," Maggie said, feeling as sad as bagpipes.

"They're so much older now," Grisha said. "Their smell must be different than when I left London."

"Does that mean you won't be able to find me when I grow up?"

"I think I would prefer not to lose you in the first place," Grisha said. "That way I won't ever have to find you."

"That's an excellent plan," Maggie said. "Don't lose me and I won't lose you."

"Agreed," he said.

"If Ella and Rachel still live here," Maggie said, "they'll be listed in the phone book."

"So we need a bookstore?" Grisha asked, and Maggie realized that of course he had never used either a phone book or a phone.

"We want a hotel," Maggie said, thinking of a lobby with pay phones.

They walked until they found a nice hotel, and, in the lobby, Maggie located a pay phone with a phonebook. There was a listing for a *Merdinger, E.,* and with the help of a map, she and Grisha found their way to the street where *Merdinger, E.* lived.

Once-elegant homes, now converted to flats, competed for sidewalk space with small squares of dirt in which tired flowers and skinny trees tried to grow.

"I think I can smell them," Grisha said, for a faint hint of the scent he had followed out of London so many years ago hung in the air. "But it might just be that we're close to the Royal College of Music."

Where Esther taught! They had to be close, Maggie thought. They just had to be.

Grisha drew some more air into his mouth. He could smell books, sheet music, biscuits, hot tea, hands worn out from years of work, and lemon thyme.

"They're here," he said, standing before number 64. "Right here."

>—•—<

A girl about Maggie's age opened the door. Her face held such a mixture of alarm and delight that it seemed they had found someone in London who could see Grisha.

"Yes, may I help you?" the girl asked, still staring.

"I hope so," Maggie said. "Does Ella or Rachel Merdinger live here?"

"Ella Merdinger does," the girl said. "She's my gran. May I say who is calling?"

"Maggie Miklós," Maggie said. "But she won't know me."

"Maggie Miklós and—?"

"How do you do," Grisha said politely, as soon as he realized that the girl could see him. "I am Benevolentia Gaudium."

"I'm Nadia," the girl said.

"Oh, thank goodness you can see him," Maggie said.

"Well, he is rather large," Nadia said, looking a bit puzzled.

Grisha, who had not scaled down to a proper size for the house, immediately did so.

"Neat," Nadia said.

"It's just that no one has been able to see us," Maggie said. "Grisha—I mean Benevolentia Gaudium—said no one in London can see a dragon."

"Well, I'm kind of odd," Nadia told them, with no trace of embarrassment. "Gran says I'm like her, so she'll probably be able to see Mr. Gaudium too."

"Please call me Grisha," Grisha said. "I knew Ella and Rachel even before they were your age."

"Then you'd best come in and have some tea," said Nadia.

The particular British habit of offering a cup of tea at every occasion (waking up, coming home, reading the paper, and, apparently, greeting a strange dragon and his friend) was one that Yakov had often remarked upon to

Grisha. The clients he liked best, Yakov would say, were the ones who asked for whiskey instead of tea.

"We would love some tea," Grisha said, smiling at the memory of his old friend. "How very kind you are."

"My great-aunt is here as well," Nadia said.

"Rachel!" Maggie exclaimed. "Grisha, Rachel!"

"You might want to call her Dr. Merdinger," Nadia said. "She's more formal than my gran is."

A doctor, Grisha thought, remembering the mischievous girl he'd known who'd come back to London after the Blitz so dedicated to her studies.

"And what, may I ask, does your gran do?" Had Ella remained serious and quiet?

"She's a music teacher and a pianist," Nadia said. "I'm actually named after my great-gran's piano teacher."

Little Ella had followed in her mother's footsteps. All those hours practicing the piano had paid off. How wonderful.

They walked with Nadia down a narrow hall lined with photographs and paintings. Next was a sitting room large enough for a grand piano. They entered the kitchen, which was small but cozy. At a round table by the window sat two elderly ladies, a Brown Betty teapot, cups, and saucers between them.

One of them—thin and regal—stood up immediately, saying, "Oh, my, oh, my."

There was no mistaking her. It was the serious girl from long ago, the one who had followed her older sister into each day with a little caution.

"Ella," Grisha said, feeling a bit awkward. "Hello."

"What is it?" asked the other woman, who was short and plump, with a face full of laughter. She did not get up, and, studying Maggie, asked, "Who are you?"

"I'm Maggie," Maggie said. "Maggie Miklós."

Ella had crossed over to Grisha and took hold of his front paws, not caring that his scales might scratch her. "I never thought I'd see you again," she said. "I was so cross that you had left before Rachel and I came home. The minute you were gone, I knew you had been real."

"Ella, are you ill?" Rachel asked. "Nadia, help your grandmother to sit down. I think the heat may have gotten to her."

"I'm sorry about your parents," Grisha said to Ella. "I loved them so. I can't imagine how hard it was to lose them."

"It *was* hard," Ella said.

"Ella," Rachel said, getting up and pushing past Maggie and Nadia. "Are you having a stroke? Who on earth do you imagine you are talking to?"

Ella wiped her eyes and turned toward her sister with a sad smile. "It's Grisha," she said.

"Aunt Rachel, you can't see him?" Nadia asked. "He's right in front of you. Here." She took hold of Rachel's hand and tried to place it on one of Grisha's scales, but he moved back a bit. The last thing he wanted was to give Rachel a shock.

"Sometimes people can't remember how to see me," he said.

"The dragon is here?" Rachel asked.

"Yes, it's Papa's teapot," Ella said to her sister. "He's come back."

"I'm sorry," Rachel said to the space where she thought Grisha might be. "It's been such a long time. . . ."

"It's been just as long for Gran," Nadia said.

"I'm out of practice, is all," Rachel said. "Too much time as a scientist and not enough as a musician like your gran."

"You were and are a marvelous doctor," Ella said.

"What do your jobs have to do with seeing a dragon who almost hits the ceiling he's so tall?" Nadia asked.

"To see a dragon or any magic requires that you think of what *might* be," Ella said. "Music is all about possibility, while medicine very practically asks you to find what *is*."

"Tell Grisha to stay a while," Rachel said. "Maybe I'll remember how to see him."

"Please tell your aunt that it's perfectly okay that she can't see me," Grisha said to Nadia.

"She's not deaf, just old," Nadia said. "Don't be rude."

"He isn't," Maggie said. "If Rachel can't see him, she can't hear him either."

"Oh," Nadia said. "I see."

"You'll have to translate," Grisha said.

"We'll all translate," Ella said. "Let's have tea."

"Nadia, open the chocolate biscuits," Rachel said. "It's not every day that a strange girl and a dragon come to tea."

Nadia and Ella got out extra cups and plates, poured tea, and passed biscuits.

"What's brought you all this way?" Rachel asked, after finding out that their guests had traveled from Vienna.

Maggie and Grisha looked at each other. He wondered where to begin and she worried about discussing a quest with a woman who couldn't even see a dragon.

"Your father's green bottles," Grisha said, deciding to get right to it. He and Maggie told the story of Leopold Lashkovic, Yakov's two potions, and the dragons who were buried somewhere in Vienna.

222

Nadia, unlike Grisha, loved *Once upon a time* stories and kept interrupting to say, in the most hopeful voice, "That happened? Really?"

Ella and Rachel, who had lived long enough to see much of the world's cruelty, listened in grim silence, breaking it only to say "Horrible" or "Oh, no."

"We've spoken with the woman who is in charge of Vienna's dragons," Maggie said. She'd noticed that Grisha had left out all mention of enchanted cats and did likewise. "If we find a potion, she will help us find the dragons."

"We were hoping that there might be some of your father's potion left in one of the bottles," Grisha said.

"Oh, dear," Rachel said. "And you've come such a long way."

"There's nothing in them," Ella said. "Only dust."

Maggie swallowed hard and put her hand on Grisha's orange scale. Oh, no. No.

"What do we remember about Papa's magic?" Ella asked. "It was so important to him."

"He had an old friend from those days," Rachel said. "Whenever he came to visit there was iced fruit cake for tea, do you remember?"

"Henrik Toov," Ella said. "He smoked pipes and then the whole house smelled."

"Yes, Dr. Toov," Rachel said. "He and Papa spoke all the time about two rivers. For hours they would go back and forth."

"Yes, yes!" Ella said. "They would argue about whether it was even worth mixing a potion or creating a compound if you didn't use water from one of those rivers."

"Didn't Dr. Toov travel to Germany every year to bring back water for his shop?" Rachel asked. "Imagine, all that way for river water. What were those rivers called?"

"The Bird and the Bragg?" Ella asked. "Brick and Branch?"

"The Breg and the Brigach," Grisha said, with a laugh. "Everyone always argued over which river was the purest."

"Everyone?" Nadia asked. "I've never heard of either river."

"Everyone who lived in the forest," Grisha explained. "The magic that people thought was in a unicorn was really in those rivers. You could cure everything from a toothache to a fever to a battle wound with their water."

Nadia repeated Grisha's words to Rachel, who nodded and then said, "Perhaps if your sleeping dragons receive water from either river, they will wake up."

"That's exactly it," Grisha said, rather loudly. He was a bit mortified that he had not thought of the rivers himself and wanted more than anything to hug Rachel. But he didn't want her frightened out of her wits to find herself embraced by what she could not see.

"It couldn't be that simple," Ella said, pouring another cup of tea.

"Oh, but it could," said Grisha, feeling better and better.

Maggie could feel herself growing flushed with excitement. She had never seen Grisha so confident.

"Wasn't that the point of everything Papa believed about magic?" Rachel asked. "It was a simple art that was difficult to practice?"

"How can you believe in magic if you can't even see a dragon?" Nadia asked.

"Magic is like the sun," Rachel said crisply. "You don't believe in it. It just is."

# CHAPTER NINETEEN

# The Heart's Shadow

**Grisha's happy, contented eyes told Maggie** they had found what they needed. She had no idea how they would get to Germany, let alone collect the water, fly home, and give it to the dragons. Then there was the whole problem of asking Thisbe to give up another memory to protect them from Leopold on their way to Germany. Maggie wasn't concerned about any of that yet, because they hadn't come to London to find a solution to every problem. They'd come for a potion, and somewhere in Germany there were two rivers whose water *was* the potion.

She looked at the sisters. "Thank you for the tea," she said, feeling inadequate and suddenly aware that she could never come close to fully repaying them.

Rachel asked if they could call her parents, not wanting to let a child back out into the streets of London by herself.

"She's not alone, Auntie," Nadia said.

"Yes, I realize that, but she will appear to be alone to many, many strangers," Rachel said. "She clearly has negligent parents."

Maggie, who had often heard her father called negligent by other parents, suspected she should be offended on Alexander's behalf.

"I promise she'll be safe," Grisha said.

"Thank you so much," Maggie said to Rachel and Ella. "I . . . I'm . . . we are so grateful."

Rachel leaned down and gave Maggie a hug, saying, "Please be careful. It's possible that waking up a host of drugged dragons will be more dangerous than you think."

Maggie nodded without believing her. After all, hadn't the most dangerous member of Leopold Lashkovic's dangerous enchanted cats turned out to be the most helpful?

"Do you think we can get enough water in a single trip?" Maggie asked, once she and Grisha were alone. "Or will we have to go to Germany over and over? Can we go right now?"

"No, I promised your father there would be no detours," Grisha said, "and that I would bring you right home from London."

Maggie sighed, for of course that was exactly the sort of thing her father would want. Now they would have to go all the way home, get permission from Alexander, and then beg Thisbe for another favor. Not to mention find a huge container for water. How much water would they need, anyway?

"Are you feeling all right?" Grisha asked. "You look a bit paler than usual."

"I'm hungry and I have to pee," she admitted, disappointed that bathrooms, eating, and other mundane details of daily life hadn't vanished because she was on a heroic quest.

They found clean bathrooms at a bistro where they ordered a good meal of cheese toast and toffee pudding with whipped cream (for her) and cabbage with fried potatoes (for him).

"I don't want to go home," Maggie said. "Let's go to the forest and get the water now."

"But Thisbe was very clear. Find the potion and then find Tyr."

"But we haven't found it yet," Maggie said. "That's why we should go to Germany now!"

"We know where the potion is, but the magic cat is another matter," Grisha said. "We're going to have to ask Kator, but I . . ."

He trailed off and Maggie stopped scraping the last bite off of her pudding plate.

"What?"

"Kator has been on every quest imaginable," Grisha said, after a long pause. "I want my one quest to be mine that I share with you. Not something that Kator takes over."

Maggie understood completely. "We'll find Tyr without Kator," she said. "And then we'll go to Germany."

>--<

"I'm glad you're back in one piece," Alexander said, after hearing the details of how they had tracked down Rachel and Ella. "I hadn't realized how much I would miss my imaginative girl and her free spirit."

"Papa, you can see Grisha, right?" Maggie asked. "You aren't pretending, are you?"

"No, of course not," he said. "Did the pianist in London worry you?"

"The doctor," Maggie said. "It's as if she forgot how to be . . . herself. Will that happen to me if I become a doctor?" She had no interest in medicine, but thought she'd like to eliminate any profession that might mean no longer being able to see or talk with Grisha.

"You and I are cut from the same cloth," Alexander said. "We do not forget what is important to us, no matter what we do."

Maggie considered her father carefully. Normally, he told her how much like her beautiful, famous mother she was, which she knew was not true. She wondered if she and Alexander really were the same. He had a sharp, elegant face and was tall and thin. Maggie did not think of herself as either elegant or beautiful. Rather she was sharp and not sharp.

"Papa, I have to find a missing cat now. And I don't know where to look."

"Is the cat part of your quest?" he asked. "The potion's not enough?"

"We need the cat so we can use the potion," Maggie said. "She was in danger so she couldn't go home, and no one knows where she is."

"If I were a cat who needed a hiding place," he said, slowly, "I would go to Rome and become one of many."

"You mean hide in plain sight?"

"Yes," Alexander said, closing his bag. "I'm off. Give me a hug."

Maggie was glad to. As wonderful as flying to London without him had been, it was just as nice to come home.

"Order some breakfast and have a nap," he said, leaving a kiss on the top of her head. "I've left you a Latin translation and four pages of math problems."

Maggie sat down at her desk and looked at her work in dismay. She was not interested in Latin and math. She needed to know where to find Tyr.

Rome was where Leopold was. Surely Tyr would not have gone there? A cat in Vienna could hide in plain sight as well.

>—•—<

When Grisha arrived at the Hotel Sacher, he discovered that his charge had spent all day in her room, ignoring her books and staring out the window. He had to say her name three times before she looked up at him.

"Oh, hello," she said. "I've been making a list of places to look for a cat in Vienna: hotels, palaces, and museums."

"If I were a cat, I'd live in Rome," Grisha said, laughing. "It's warmer, and everyone there loves cats."

"Did you say Rome?" He nodded, slightly alarmed at how bright her eyes had become.

"That's exactly what Papa said. We should go. It's a sign!"

"No, it's not," he said. "Thisbe thinks Tyr is near Kator or somewhere in this city."

"Let's start looking," Maggie said. She ripped a page from her notebook. "These are the kind of places where Vienna's cats live."

Three days and many hotels, palaces, and museums later, they had to admit defeat. It wasn't that they hadn't found cats in each of these places. As was expected in Vienna, each place had a proud and snotty cat, each of them deeply indifferent to questions about Tyr.

Maggie and Grisha even went to the university to track down the cat who'd scratched her all those years ago. They'd found him in the economics building. "I don't go to the poetry offices anymore," he told Grisha, sniffing. "And I certainly haven't seen a cat with a short, bushy tail."

Exhausted and empty-handed, Grisha and Maggie retreated to the lobby of the Sacher. They sat in plush chairs and ordered a plate of cookies that they were too disappointed to eat.

"I really don't think Tyr would go to Rome," Grisha said. He knew by now that Maggie liked to jump ahead to the next step.

"Tyr would have every reason," Maggie said. "What better place than a city known to welcome cats?"

"I just don't think she would risk being that close to Leopold," Grisha said. "And we certainly shouldn't either."

"I thought Leopold lived in a villa outside of Rome," she said.

"Yes, but—"

"Papa will go with us," she said, firmly. "And if Leopold discovers we are in Rome, it will look as if you're there as part of your job and that I'm traveling with my father. Not as if we are looking for Tyr."

Grisha did see the wisdom of going to a city that had the largest population of cats in all of Europe. But he knew that the danger involved in going to Rome was not a stupid one, easily avoided. Every quest will naturally be different from the others that have come before it, but no quest worthy of its name will allow you to hide from your biggest fear.

Alexander, it seemed to Maggie, agreed all too quickly to take them both to Rome. At first she thought it was because he did not want to risk losing another argument about her travels. But when he said, "Rome is where Antiquity took root when the Greeks faded away," she realized that the price she would pay for being allowed to search for Tyr would be a huge number of art and history lessons.

Maggie loved her father and suspected that she herself would probably become the sort of grown-up who loved sentences that began with "Rome is where Antiquity took root." However, she was beginning to think that her education was interfering with the sort of person she wanted to be right now. She did not want to go to Rome because of Antiquity. She wanted to go because of buried dragons and enchanted cats.

All she said to her father, however, was, "That sounds nice."

>—•—<

When they arrived in Rome, they went to an apartment that Alexander's friend Matan Bassani had loaned him for a few days. Maggie had met Matan many times during his visits to Vienna and never liked the way he always murmured *So like your mother.* I'm glad he's out of town, she thought, while walking up six flights of stairs to the top floor of a small, elegant building.

Everywhere in the apartment there were windows with balconies, floor-to-ceiling bookcases, or beautiful objects. By the doorway were two lamps in the shape of elephants and a large, brightly colored glass vase. There was a chandelier hanging from the ceiling and, on the floor, the sort of beautiful rug people are afraid to step on.

Maggie and Grisha stood quietly in the massive front hall.

For the first time in her life, Maggie wondered about the apartment in Vienna where she had lived with her parents before her mother died. Of course it wouldn't have been anything like this one, which was grand and formal and felt a bit like a hotel lobby. But the Vienna apartment, which was the last place her mother had called home, must have had tall windows and bookcases for all of Papa's books. And perhaps even some pretty objects.

Had it had balconies as well?

"Maggie, come here," her father called. "I want to show you something."

She and Grisha wandered through the apartment's huge rooms, not finding Alexander until they got to a small alcove tucked into a corner of the dining room. It was empty except that on its curved wall hung five small paintings in various shades of blue and silver.

These were from a series Caroline had done when she was pregnant. Maggie had read about them in art books and magazine articles, but up until this moment, had seen them only in photographs. She had not realized that they looked as if the colors were moving. They shimmered with their blues and silvers.

"Oh, my," Grisha said, his voice as soft and whispery as a dragon's could get.

"Can I touch?" Maggie asked her father, and he nodded.

The only other paintings of her mother's that Maggie remembered seeing this close had been three of the most famous—huge canvases covered in angular shapes of black, brown, and orange—and she'd been uncomfortable to find that she didn't like them. But these small paintings were somehow different, and as Maggie put her hand against the surface of the one that seemed to shimmer the most, a word she'd never thought to use crept out from behind the shadow of her heart: *Mama.*

In just that moment, she felt the soft undersides of Grisha's paws settle on her shoulders. No one said anything. Finally, she took her hand away from the painting and, still silent, hugged her father before going back out into the huge and beautiful apartment.

>—•—<

When Maggie and Alexander went to bed, Grisha curled up on the cool tile floor of one of the front hall's balconies, all of which overlooked a small park. Soon Maggie joined him.

"I can't sleep," she said. "When I close my eyes all I see are blue and silver colors."

"From the paintings?" he asked.

She nodded. "Until I saw those paintings, I never really thought about how Mama was once alive."

"Do you want me to tuck you into bed?" Grisha asked, wondering if that would help her feel a bit less sad.

"No, I'm not at all sleepy," she said. "And it's not just the paintings. How are we ever going to find Tyr? The city is huge, and Papa has an endless list of things we *have* to see."

Grisha laughed. He had seen the list, which was rather endless. A bit of smoke puffed out of his nose and floated up into the dark sky.

"The more of Rome we see," he said, "the more cats we'll see."

"You're going to ask stray cats if they know Tyr?" Maggie asked. "I thought you would smell for her."

"We'll do a little of both."

"And how do you smell for a cat you've never met?" Maggie asked.

"It's more that if Tyr is here, I will smell a bit of Thisbe. We carry the smell of those we have loved with us," Grisha said. "We never lose that."

"I hope that's true," Maggie said, and pressed her nose against her wrist. Was it possible she smelled like the famous and dead Caroline Brooks, who had also been her mother?

# CHAPTER TWENTY

# EXILED

**THE NEXT AFTERNOON, AFTER ENTIRELY TOO MANY**
museums and churches, Alexander had an appointment
with his Italian publisher. He said he would meet Maggie
and Grisha in two hours at the café across the piazza from
the church of Santa Maria Maggiore.

Maggie was tired and her brain hurt from trying to
keep straight all of the information Alexander had been
trying to cram into it as he took her and Grisha around
Rome, giving mini lectures on history, art, religion, and
the fact that the pope had once had two armies.

"And five dragons on retainer," Grisha had added,
a bit of information that, much to Maggie's delight, had
prevented Alexander from speaking for a full two minutes.

"You should rest," Grisha told Maggie now. "I can go
places you can't because no one in Rome notices me."

Maggie only agreed when he pointed out that stray cats might talk more freely with a fellow four-footed creature than with a human girl. She refused to go back to the apartment, not wanting to nap in spite of being exhausted. Instead, she settled at a table outside the café near the church and ordered a chocolate ice.

Her eyes felt dry and scratchy, but every time she closed them, she saw only blues and silvers mixed up together. It was as if her feelings, normally things that behaved in an orderly manner, were now all jumbled and projecting paintings upon her eyelids. As well as questions with no answers.

For example, if her mother were still alive, would she be willing to help find and free the dragons? Her father had done more than just hire Grisha or give his permission. Alexander seemed to truly admire and respect Grisha, and at the very least, he could *see* Grisha—but had her mother seen Vienna's dragons? Did she take time to notice, to spend time on things that didn't belong? Maggie had to wonder if she would even have met Grisha in the first place if her mother were alive. Caroline had preferred Berlin to every other city in Europe and had lived in Vienna only because of Alexander's job.

Maggie was nervous and uncomfortable at having so many thoughts about her mother. She tried to make a list of everything Alexander had said earlier in the day that was important for an educated person to know. Instead, she found herself wondering whether her parents had ever been in Rome together and when. She closed her eyes again, hoping to empty her mind, but it immediately filled up with blues and silvers.

"Crap," Maggie said aloud, squeezing her eyes shut as tightly as possible. It was a word Alexander particularly disliked, as he always said that vulgar language reflected boring thoughts. "Crap, crap, crap."

"Your parents visited Rome many times," a voice said. "In fact, you were with them the last time they were here. It was the week of your third birthday."

Maggie's eyes flew open. At a table a few feet away from hers was an old man in a wheelchair. Although it was a warm day, he was wearing a heavy coat and a blanket covered his legs.

"You have memories of that trip," the man said, wheeling himself over to her table. "You have memories of your mother too, but you have no idea where they are."

The man stopped so that his chair was uncomfortably close to hers. He had eyes so dark that they seemed entirely black, which Maggie knew was impossible. "But I know how to find them," he said. "And I could give them to you."

Maggie looked at the man's face. He did not look that old, in spite of his white hair and the wheelchair. The irises of his eyes were black, and the white parts were not white but a greenish yellow. Part of Maggie wanted to get up and run far away, but most of her wanted to stay. Whoever this was, he was from the world of magic. He was part of why she and Grisha had come to Rome.

"I understand you have met my Theodora and have seen what a terrible thing it is to have lost your memories," the man said. "Poor, silly creature has no idea that she even lost them. I broke the neck of her dearest friend, and yet she still hugs me whenever we meet." He gave a horrible, dry laugh that sounded like a cough.

Maggie's back tightened up so much that she was sure she couldn't move.

"You, however, know exactly what memories you *don't* have," the man said, his black eyes shining like polished gems. "Imagine how marvelous it might be if you could have them. A woman as lovely and talented as your mother should be remembered by her only child."

"Leopold," Maggie said, not having meant to speak at all. Had he known her mother?

"Miss Miklós," the old man said, bowing in his chair. "A pleasure."

So this was Leopold. Leopold Lashkovic himself was sitting right next to her. It was strange, terrifying, and marvelous all at once. He had captured Grisha, buried dragons, and had killed one of his own cats. And yet Leopold was also a man with hands that had spots and wrinkles. His eyes, while frightening, had lashes and lids just like regular eyes did. The fact that she was merely nervous when she should be terrified was odd, but also soothing.

"My young friend Gregory is an excellent spy," Leopold said. "He keeps me informed of anything my traitorous felines forget to mention."

Maggie, who might have remained silent otherwise, sprang into action at the implied criticism of Thisbe's behavior. "She told me nothing I didn't know already," she said in as crisp a formal tone as she could manage. "Both Thisbe and Theodora have refused to help me and have warned Grisha—DR87, that is—not to do anything. So he hasn't. We are here with my father. That is all."

"Calm yourself, Miss Miklós," Leopold said. "My cats are not in any trouble with me, but I myself have much to fear if you manage to wake those lost, slumbering dragons."

"You buried dragons who had done nothing wrong," Maggie said. "You ruined their lives with a spell that made

245

them leave their forest. You should be happy at the idea of setting them free."

"You understand nothing," Leopold said, and the bitterness in his voice cut through the air like a sword, making Maggie flinch. He turned toward a waiter, who most certainly had not been there a second before, and said, "Brandy and a mineral water, along with some cookies for the young lady."

The waiter murmured, "Here you are, sir," and the food simply appeared on the table. It all happened so smoothly and quickly that Maggie had no time to be alarmed or surprised. She watched Leopold sip from his brandy glass before she bit into one of the cookies. It was filled with sugared almond paste—her favorite.

"Your whole future is waiting for you, but I am an old man," Leopold said. "I live in exile from all I hold dear. Happiness is no longer mine to claim."

Maggie had always thought of being happy as something you were, not something you claimed.

"But I am still alive," Leopold continued, "and those dragons are buried as the result of my magic. If you reverse my work, I may die."

The cookie in Maggie's mouth suddenly tasted like wet cotton. If Leopold thought she was trying to kill him, who knew what he might do to her? She could feel her legs shaking under the table and she slipped her hands, also shaking, into her lap where he couldn't see them.

"I can't force you to abandon your plans," he said. "But perhaps I can persuade you."

"I mean you no harm," Maggie said. "But those dragons have the right to be free."

"As do we all," Leopold said, moving his hands in front of Maggie. "Close your eyes."

Without meaning to, she did. Instead of seeing blue and silver or simply darkness, Maggie saw a large, messy room with easels and a table covered in buckets of paint. A slim, elegant woman, dressed in slacks and a smock, was kneeling and talking to a very small child. The child had brown hair and large eyes; her hands were covered in yellow and orange paint, and she was smearing her bright, sticky fingers across paper taped to the floor.

The woman, whom Maggie recognized from photographs, was reaching out to pat the child gently on the face, and—

"Show's over, dear."

The vision vanished.

Maggie's eyes flew open. She knew that what she had seen had actually happened. She'd been with her mother in her studio. They had laughed and played and painted together. It was a memory she'd been far too young to remember, but it still existed somewhere inside of her.

"The afternoons you spent in her studio were your favorite times," Leopold said. "But there are also countless other memories of her putting you to bed, teaching you to read, playing peekaboo, and singing silly songs. All yours for a special one-time price."

"How do you know this? How did you do that?" Maggie asked. What she meant was *Do it again, please do it again; I have to go back there.*

A smug, satisfied expression crept across the old man's face. "I may be weak, but the taking and giving of your memory is still well within my grasp."

"But those are *my* memories. You said so yourself!" Maggie cried, opening and closing her eyes again and again, hoping to see her mother. But now there was only darkness.

"Yes, the memories are yours," Leopold told her. "But letting you see them is up to me."

The memory of her mother had felt as if they had actually been together. She *had* known her mother and *had* loved her. The grief she always said she couldn't have for someone she didn't recall was, Maggie saw now, an endless sorrow over not having had the chance to save those memories.

Someday, her father would die, and all she'd have left would be her memories of him. Wouldn't she do anything in the world to keep them? Should she, then, do anything to gain access to memories of her mother? Maggie felt her mouth go as dry and scratchy as her eyes. And then suddenly her eyes, throat, and nose were full of smoke and heat. A blast of fire shot across the piazza, incinerating her cookies and Leopold's brandy.

"Get away from her." Grisha's voice boomed, thick and menacing. "Get away!"

The dragon was loping across the square, snorting balls of fire that landed all around Leopold's wheelchair. Leopold put his hand over each ball and Maggie watched them fizzle out as if doused with water.

She stood up and placed herself between Grisha and Leopold. "It's okay," she said. "He's not threatening me."

"I don't want him near you," Grisha said. "It's not safe."

"Benevolentia Gaudium," Leopold said. "My lost friend."

"Not one word," Grisha said to him. To Maggie, he said, "He's not to be trusted."

"He showed me my mother," she said. "I remembered her."

"You could remember her touch," Leopold said softly. "How much is that worth to you?"

"I know you," Grisha said to Leopold. "You are just as likely to take away what you promise to give."

"Calm yourself and come sit," Leopold said. "The three of us share a bond. That makes it likely we can reach a bargain."

Grisha forced himself to remain calm. What would be best for Maggie? For their quest? He took a deep breath and then scaled down considerably; he'd been almost as big as the Church of Santa Maria Maggiore. He sat down in a chair between Maggie and Leopold.

"We do not have a bond," he said, his voice still bigger than Maggie had ever heard.

"You and I certainly do," Leopold said. "We are exiled from the lives we once had and from a world that no longer exists."

Maggie knew that was true for Grisha and all of Vienna's dragons. She realized that it must also be true for the old man with strange eyes and waning powers.

"Leave Maggie out of it," Grisha said. "Whatever it is you want, bargain with me."

"I've nothing to offer," Leopold said. "I can never return the years I stole from you."

"You could make up for it by telling us how to find the dragons you buried," Maggie said.

"Young lady, if I help you with that, I will hasten my own death," Leopold told her. "And I still enjoy being alive." He leaned across the table and touched Maggie's arm. "I will give you your memories if you stop looking for Tyr."

"I will not let you cast a spell that involves her memories," Grisha said.

"I have nothing else to offer her," Leopold said. "And I want to live."

"Everybody wants to live," Maggie said. "For example, the dragons you buried would much rather live than remain buried and forgotten."

"You would have your memories of your mother and not have to rely on knowing her through the paintings."

Something about that nagged at Maggie. It reminded her of something her father often said, but she couldn't think what.

"All you have to do is stop looking for Tyr," Leopold said. "Do the wise thing and give up. Let an old man live in peace. It's the easier way for you both."

"We're close to finding Tyr, aren't we?" Grisha asked, realizing. "We must be very close."

"I've no idea," Leopold said. "I've always assumed that she died."

The old sorcerer spoke with such forced lightness that Grisha knew he must be lying. "If we weren't close to finding her, you wouldn't be trying to blackmail Maggie into giving up."

"Caroline Brooks was your mother, and you have the right to remember her," Leopold told Maggie. "Consider carefully what you choose to do."

Just then Maggie remembered what it was her father often said—that someday she would come to know Caroline through her paintings. And he was right, of course. It had been while in front of the blue-and-silver paintings that she'd had her first real feelings about her mother. The word—*Mama*—had come as if it were a gift, straight from the paintings.

"I won't take your bribe," Maggie said. "She was my mother, so those memories aren't yours to give. Knowing I have them is enough for me."

Dark sparks shot from Leopold's very dark eyes. "You are a stupid, stupid girl, and your friend here is just as worthless," he said. And with those words, Leopold and his wheelchair turned into seven cats. It happened as smoothly and quickly as when the brandy and cookies had appeared on the table.

The cats were skinny things; hungry looks in their coal-black eyes with thick greenish-yellow rims. Two rubbed up against Maggie's ankles and the other five circled Grisha.

"Run!" Grisha called out, but it was too late—both cats had sunk their teeth into her heels.

A sharp stinging spread across her feet, feeling like the worst scrape imaginable, but even more dismaying was the sight of blood oozing from Grisha's back paws and tail.

Grisha shot fire at the two cats who'd bitten Maggie. Immediately, all seven cats scampered away across the piazza, in a single file line.

The stinging at her heels gave way to a warm, wet feeling as blood made its way out of the puncture marks. "Crap," Maggie said, because what else could you say after being bitten by an ancient artisan in the shape of seven cats?

# CHAPTER TWENTY-ONE

# FIRSTS

GRISHA HAD IMMEDIATELY PUT HIS PAWS AND THEN his tail into his mouth to remove whatever poison the cats might have transmitted. He quickly did the same with Maggie's feet. She thought it was disgusting and ticklish in equal measure. Since no one could see Grisha (in this way, Rome was a lot like London), no one saw why she was standing on one foot, holding up the other one. She was torn between laughing at what he was doing and crying at how much her bites stung.

She asked him if it wasn't an old wives' tale about curing snakebite by sucking out the venom. "Not if a dragon does it," he said. "My mouth has so much fire going in and out that it's as close to sterile as you can get."

"Do you think Leopold wanted to kill us?" Maggie asked.

"He certainly didn't want us to live," Grisha said. "But he's too weak to kill us."

Grisha had been shocked to see how much Leopold had changed. His spotted, wrinkled hands, which had once been porcelain smooth, betrayed how much power the old man had lost. Unlike men, sorcerers did not age, but they decayed as their power faded. Once he knew Maggie was okay, he listened to her argument that they tell Alexander an angry stray cat had bitten her.

"I don't want to tell him about magical cats and people being turned into bugs," she said. "He's a bit vague about the whole Leopold part of our quest, and if he finds out everything I'll get a huge lecture."

"We don't lie to your father," Grisha said. "Our quest is an honorable one. Lying is for cowards."

"Yes, of course," Maggie said. "But it's hard to live up to things like honor when you are only eleven and need permission to go to Germany."

"You do have a point," Grisha said. "He won't let you go anywhere if he thinks you're in danger of another attack."

"I'll tell him it was one cat, which is a small lie," she said. "But it's a lie for a good reason."

"We have to find Tyr before we can plan to go to Germany," Grisha reminded her.

"I thought you said we must be close to finding her," Maggie said.

"Close is not the same as finding," Grisha said.

"Did you get any clues from talking to cats?"

"No," Grisha said. "No one has seen or smelled a cat with an odd tail."

>—•—<

When Alexander met them, he looked long and hard at the table with its charred remains of a brandy glass and a plate of cookies. "Anyone want to tell me what happened?" he asked, his voice both quieter and calmer than usual.

Grisha watched the poet's face as Maggie stuttered through her story of an angry stray cat. She was not a terribly good liar and kept switching back and forth between it being one cat and then three cats. In one version, she had accidentally kicked one of the cats, and in the other, a single cat had bitten her for no reason at all.

"That's not it," Grisha said, very uncomfortable with the lying they were doing.

"I didn't think so," Alexander said, and sat quietly while the story of Leopold, the offer of retrieving lost memories, and the seven cats spilled forth. "I see," he said at one point. Also, "Is that so?"

Grisha, like Maggie, knew that when Alexander was very calm, he was the most upset.

"I'm certainly glad Leopold is not that powerful anymore," Alexander said, once he was sure he understood them. "But let's get you to a doctor for antibiotics and a proper exam."

Maggie tried to explain why that was unnecessary because of Grisha's sterile mouth, but her father was insistent, saying, "I believe in taking little girls who have been bitten by a seven-cat-sized sorcerer to the doctor."

Grisha saw with relief that Maggie was too tired to argue, though he knew that if any poison had reached her blood, no antibiotic would help. Still, he was glad to have a doctor take a look at her bite marks, which were very red and swollen.

Unfortunately for Maggie, the doctor decided that she did need a rabies shot, which Grisha whispered to her was going to hurt and that he was so sorry but there was no getting around it.

The two separate shots, delivered by very long and alarming needles, went right into her heels. Although Grisha could see that Maggie was trying to be brave, she burst into tears and pressed her face against her father's shoulder.

"God forgive me," Alexander said. "Until right now, I have always liked cats."

"You can still like them, Papa," Maggie said. "Just not enchanted ones."

*Enchanted.*

And all became as clear as glass to Grisha. The importance of Leopold's changed hands and the yellow-green in his eyes fell into place.

All this time, Grisha had been asking cats about a cat with a short, bushy tail. But Tyr had given up her powers *before* Thisbe gave up ever seeing her again. So Thisbe had never seen Tyr *after* she no longer had powers.

Bells, Grisha thought, using the worst word he knew. Tyr was no longer enchanted, he realized, so she'd have a perfectly normal tail. I should've asked if there were a cat who didn't seem to know how normal cats behaved. Or who was heartbroken.

Alexander had been heartbroken when his wife died, and what had he done? He'd remained in Vienna and, every chance he had, he had visited Caroline's paintings, which hung in museums, galleries, and homes. In other words, he'd stayed close to what reminded him of what he'd lost.

Grisha couldn't believe he hadn't figured it out sooner. That's why Thisbe had said to ask Kator where

Tyr was. It wasn't because Kator knew where she was, but that Tyr would have stayed close to the dragon who had once guarded her.

He and Maggie had been looking for a needle in a haystack, when they should have seen that the needle had been near them all along. They weren't looking for an unknown cat, but for the cat he'd seen with Alexander at the library: the one who was occasionally at the Blaue Bar.

Grisha decided to wait until they were safely home in Vienna before telling Maggie of his suspicion. He saw no point in taking a chance that Leopold might still be skulking around them in the form of some cat or another, listening and watching.

>—•—<

Once she returned to her room at the Sacher, Maggie pinned up a postcard of her mother's blue-and-silver paintings. She didn't want to dwell on her dead mother, but neither was there any point in pretending that she didn't miss her. The postcard would be a reminder of what she wished she remembered about the mother she'd lost.

Memory was such an odd and unfair thing, she thought. She'd never need a reminder of Grisha galloping across the piazza, shooting fire at Leopold.

"We might never find Tyr," Maggie told Grisha, "but you have already done a heroic deed."

Grisha's whole body glowed like the dying embers of a fire with embarrassment and pride. Even though Maggie wasn't a princess in a prison, he had confronted danger to protect his friend and ally. *That* was something a dragon could boast about. Finally, Grisha could brag at the bar along with the others.

"I've been thinking," Grisha started. "What if Tyr has found us?"

"What do you mean?" Maggie bounded across the room until there was hardly any space between them. "Did you find something out?"

"Well, it was more what I didn't find out."

"Tell me!"

"I think Tyr is the cat who follows your father," Grisha told her. "The one who lives at the Sacher?"

"That scraggly thing?" Maggie asked. "She has a perfectly ordinary tail."

"So would Tyr," Grisha said. "When I first knew Leopold, his eyes were completely black and his hands looked like they were made of porcelain."

"Well, Leopold's hands are old because now he's old," Maggie said. "But those eyes are really dark, Grisha. They're darker than Thisbe's."

"But the part around the edges is no longer all black."

That was true, Maggie thought, thinking of the icky greenish-yellow color she'd seen in Leopold's eyes. "So you think Tyr might look normal now?" she asked.

"Maybe not *normal* normal," Grisha said. "But as normal as an enchanted cat who lost all her powers can be."

Maggie thought about the little cat she'd spent years ignoring. The creature never accepted any affection and only ate food if Kurt put it on a white-and-gold cake plate. She'd seen the cat at the hotel and at the university and just sauntering down the wide boulevard behind the Opera House. That cat was as normal a part of her day as the Hotel Sacher itself.

"But I thought each of Leopold's cats had that odd tail."

"Since Tyr had given up her magic, she won't show any signs of being enchanted. And that's all the tail is."

"But wouldn't Kator have seen Tyr at the bar?" she asked. "And then told all of you that one of Leopold's cats was now quite harmless?"

"It's possible that the spell Thisbe cast to keep Tyr safe was so strong that no one who knew her can see her anymore," Grisha said. "Remember that Thisbe was trying to save her friend's life. And the strength of that spell could have infected anyone who had known Tyr as an enchanted cat."

"But *we* never knew Tyr," Maggie said. Her face split into such a wide smile that she could feel her skin stretching. "So *we* can see her!"

And with that, she was off, Grisha close behind, down eleven flights of stairs to the Blaue Bar in search of a cat who might be their last clue.

Tyr was not there or anywhere in the lobby. Kurt said he hadn't seen her in weeks. She wasn't at the university or in the library or any place that Alexander went. Over the next few afternoons, Maggie and Grisha walked throughout the streets surrounding the hotel looking for Tyr.

It wasn't until all of the dragons were at the Blaue Bar that they saw the white cat with colored markings. When Maggie and Grisha arrived at the bar, the "scraggly thing" was already curled up near where Alexander sat.

Maggie crawled under the table. The cat's green eyes blinked at her.

"Hello," Maggie said.

"I've been waiting a long time for you to find me," Tyr said.

Maggie wanted to throw her arms up in victory, but said, "Thisbe told me to look for you, only it took us a while to figure out where."

"It certainly did," Tyr said. "I was beginning to think you wouldn't be bright enough."

Maggie tried not to laugh or smile. A cat, she now realized, was rude just because. It wasn't personal.

>—•—<

Tyr was curious about Germany and, upon hearing the explanation, said that using water from the Black Forest was not the stupidest thing she'd ever heard. Maggie knew this was high praise coming from a cat. "Come meet my friend," she said. "He's been waiting."

At the sight of the elusive cat, Grisha let out a wisp of smoke. "We are very glad to finally meet you," he said. He had pulled up another chair and piled cushions on it so that Tyr could easily see over the top of the table.

"Thank you," Tyr said. "When you saw me in the library, it was the first time a dragon had looked at me since the night I gave up my powers."

Tyr looked over at Kator, who was loudly arguing with three other dragons about the best way to take a sword away from a man on horseback. "When I rubbed up against him, he couldn't feel it," Tyr said. "That's when I understood that Thisbe had done something."

"You were caught," Maggie said. "The guards were going to kill you."

"I figured as much," Tyr said. "And I know Thisbe meant well, but her spell to protect me has had a serious blowback."

"A blowback is the unintended consequence of a spell," Grisha told Maggie.

"Giving up my magic to free the dragons only worked halfway because Thisbe didn't give up her magic as well," Tyr continued.

"Does that mean that half of the dragons went free?" Maggie asked. She hadn't known that any part of Tyr's spell had worked.

"Not exactly," Tyr said. "I'll have to show you."

"Tonight?" Maggie asked.

"I can take you now," Tyr said.

Grisha told Maggie to get permission from her father. Certain that after what had happened in Rome, Alexander wouldn't let her go anywhere with a cat, Maggie simply interrupted her father's conversation and told him she was going to bed. She had never successfully told him a lie and was amazed at how easy it was.

# CHAPTER TWENTY-TWO

# COLORS

FOLLOWING THE LITTLE CAT, MAGGIE AND GRISHA found themselves walking a familiar path toward the Stadtpark. Maggie was sure they were heading to the Kursalon, the park's music hall that looked like a palace. But Tyr took them down to the U4 metro station. And instead of waiting on the platform for a train, they went through a heavy door that said, in German, NO ENTRANCE. They ended up in a small room filled with noisy and hot machines that were part of the *U-Bahn*'s rail system.

In the middle of the room was an unusual flight of stairs that vanished into the ground after only three steps. But when you'd taken those three steps, three more appeared. Each three-step set was very narrow and had no railings.

"Don't worry," Tyr said. "No one has died using them."

"Where do they go?" Maggie asked, not exactly comforted by the assurance.

"To the tunnels," Tyr said.

After about a hundred or so steps, Maggie got into a rhythm of only being able to see three steps at a time (the next three did not appear until you were practically done with the previous three, and then those three disappeared the minute you started on the next set).

Grisha scaled down considerably in size. "We're so close to finding them," he whispered to her. "I never thought we'd get this close."

Maggie pressed her hand against his orange scale, partly to say *I know* and partly because she did not think those stairs looked safe.

"Just follow me," Tyr said, making her way down the strange steps gracefully.

Just as she was beginning to feel comfortable using them, the stairs ended. "Thank goodness," Grisha whispered, and Maggie smiled.

As they turned this way and that, it seemed as if they were in a maze of tunnels. The farther they walked, the warmer it got.

"Who built these?" Grisha asked. The tunnel floors had the same smooth, rounded shape as the sides and the ceilings. They were oddly familiar, and he wondered where he would have seen them before now.

"The dragons built everything down here," Tyr told him.

Of course, Grisha thought. These were similar to the underground spaces dragons used to build out of dead trees, stones, and underbrush. Nothing in the forest was ever wasted, and the dragons who loved to build made beautiful underground dwellings to protect creatures from rain, ice, snow, or extreme cold.

Grisha had dropped to all fours, but Maggie had to walk with her feet wider apart than normal to keep her balance. It was as if the halls and the stairs had been designed so that anyone with two legs instead of four would have difficulty using them. On top of that, she began to have trouble breathing. The air was becoming very, very warm.

Tyr made one last turn into one last tunnel. At the end of it, Maggie and Grisha could see flickering hints of flames. As they approached the source of the fire, the smell of smoke choked the air, and suddenly they were there. The tunnel opened up into a huge, cavernous space.

And there before them, everywhere they looked, were the missing dragons.

These dragons were not quiet sleepers. The creatures who were curled up on straw beds or stretched out on old newspapers snorted, tossed, turned, and exhaled fire.

Maggie, who had only ever seen the dragons at the bar, was amazed at all of the colors spread out before her.

White, silver, black, fuchsia, turquoise, and burgundy created a mosaic of color across the floor. Wings furled and unfurled like gorgeous banners as dragons exhaled fire that quickly vanished, leaving behind heat and smoke.

Maggie wanted so much to talk to each and every one of them, to ask them about the battles they had fought, the kings they had rescued, and the dreams they'd spent the past forty years having.

"Do they ever wake up?" Grisha asked Tyr. It was wonderful to see the dragons whom he had feared were gone forever.

"No, but they aren't dying anymore, thanks to me," Tyr said. "The spell Leopold used was killing most of them. It was supposed to make them quiet, but his magic wasn't strong enough to be precise. Instead of making them quiet, they all fell asleep. A couple had a bad reaction to the spell itself and got fatally ill."

Without thinking, Grisha and Maggie moved closer to each other until they were almost touching. Watching the dragons sleep began to feel disrespectful, but to look away felt just as wrong.

"My half of the spell kept the sick dragons from dying," Tyr said. "Thisbe's half would have woken all of them up."

Maggie wondered whether she would rather not have discovered any of this. It was awful to see so much beauty trapped in a kind of living death. She made herself focus on the part that was good news: Because of Tyr, the dragons were alive. She had to hope that soon they would be awake and free.

"Where are we?" she asked, wanting to make sure that she and Grisha would be able to get back to this place even if they never saw Tyr again.

"Schönbrunn," the cat said.

Now a museum, Schönbrunn had been the emperor's summer palace as well as where he'd been born. It was a huge building with an even bigger garden. It was so big that one could easily imagine the earth beneath it absorbing a large number of dragons.

"Poor things," Maggie said. "It's so wrong."

Grisha, feeling much the same but worried about the effects of the heat on his human companion, turned to Tyr. "Take us back," he said. "We've seen enough." He did not want to return until they were able to bring all these dragons back into the world.

>—•—<

They retraced their steps to the Blaue Bar and discovered that walking up the vanishing stairs was easier than going down. To cover her lie, Maggie told her father she hadn't been able to sleep. She couldn't believe they'd been gone for less than an hour, as it felt like the universe had shifted.

"Whipped cream and cake should help," Alexander said with a smile, before turning back to his friends.

For a moment or two, Maggie stood by his table, amazed that her father and all his friends were behaving normally, as if more than seventy dragons weren't trapped under the city's earth.

"Everything is so wrong," she said to Grisha.

"Not everything," he told her. "The whole world is not horrible just because one part is."

"It *feels* horrible," she said, and he nodded. Yes, of course it did.

"Will they ever wake up?" Grisha asked Tyr.

"They might," Tyr said. "But the river water alone won't do the trick. It has to be used by someone who knows magic."

"But isn't the water like a potion?" she asked.

"It's exactly like one," Tyr said.

"Well, you can use a potion without giving anything up," Maggie said. "You don't have to know magic to use it."

"That's not true," Tyr said.

"It *is*," Maggie said. "Grisha, tell her what Yakov told you when he set you free."

Grisha briefly relayed what Yakov had said about having to give something up in order to practice magic, but that with potions, it was simply a question of finding the right one and using it.

Tyr asked whether Yakov had ever seen Grisha again after he'd left for Vienna.

"No, but I wasn't allowed to leave the city," Grisha said.

"And he never came to visit you?" Tyr asked.

"No, he didn't," Grisha said. "I always thought he might, and then I stopped hoping."

"You realize he gave up being able to see you," Tyr said matter-of-factly. "It wasn't the nettles that made the potion work."

Grisha had a sudden image of Yakov clearing his throat and wiping his eyes. His farewell words—*Wherever you go, you'll take a part of my heart*—took on a new meaning. If only he'd known. He felt stricken, sick with sadness.

But Maggie was excited. Yakov, who hadn't been a magician, had been able to make a potion work. He had given up what he loved.

Grisha, in the way friends sometimes do, realized what she was thinking and shook his head. "No, don't. Maggie, *don't*."

It would be easier, she thought, if she didn't look at him. She'd be unhappy and Grisha would be too, but together they'd have a moment of glory. After that, they wouldn't have to see each other in order to be linked forever.

"Not everyone can see dragons," Maggie said to Tyr.

"I know," the cat said. "It takes a certain sensibility to notice what is possible."

"Even people who might want to can't always do it, but I can," she said. "If I were to give up seeing dragons, I would be giving up something I love more than almost anything."

Tyr tilted her head and examined Maggie as if seeing her for the first time.

"There has to be another way," Grisha said.

"Are you sure about this?" Tyr asked Maggie.

"It's out of the question," Grisha said.

"It's your choice," Tyr said. "But to give up something that important to you, you have to be sure."

"I'm sure," Maggie said. To Grisha, she said, "It'll be like Rachel. Only instead of not being able to see you because I'm a doctor, it will be because of what we did together."

"Magic asks too much," Grisha said. "It's not fair." In his long life, he'd had much time to think about all that was wrong with magic.

"Magic asks for its exact price," Maggie reminded him. In her short life, what she'd learned about magic was that it demanded a sacrifice. This was one she believed she could make. "Even if I can't see you, you'll see me," she said.

"Will I?" Grisha asked Tyr. "Or would that be part of what she gives up?"

"I can still see Thisbe," Tyr said. "I often go to the roof of the D.E.E. just to see her."

Grisha turned back to Maggie. "Are you sure you've thought about this?"

"That's the beauty of it," she said, her words rushing out. "I don't have to think. It's the exact right thing to do."

"Being the right thing doesn't mean we won't regret doing it," the dragon said.

"Grisha, it's our quest," she said. "How could we regret that?"

Time makes you regret things, he thought. But there was no way to explain that to a human as young as Maggie. And the mix of determination and excitement in her voice and eyes was not to be taken lightly. If they regretted it, at least they would do so together.

He thought of all the sleeping dragons. "How much water do you think we should bring back from the forest?" Grisha asked Tyr, and was rewarded with the rare sight of a smiling cat.

# CHAPTER TWENTY-THREE

# FLY AWAY HOME

MAGGIE THOUGHT THE BLACK FOREST WAS DISAP-
pointingly like other forests. There were the usual trees,
birds, bugs, brambles, and rotting things. There were
sounds that were either too quiet (the slight rustle of
wind) or too loud (an angry owl or a tree branch crash-
ing). The air felt damp and heavy.

To Grisha, being in the forest was like slipping into
a bath at the end of a long day. The spell Thisbe had used
to keep Leopold from detecting a dragon in Germany
was good for only thirty-six hours, so he had to resist
the temptation to detour in search of his favorite trees.
Instead, he ate an acorn from every oak tree they passed.

><·<

Grisha and Maggie had answered all of Thisbe's many
questions about Tyr. Once they'd reassured her at least

four times that the small cat was well, Thisbe had set to work on getting them to Germany. "I'll give up three memories of Tatiana to keep your trip secret from Leopold. One memory for every twelve hours," she said.

"Is there another way?" Maggie asked, not wanting to be responsible for that type of loss.

"There isn't, and anyway, it's fitting—Leopold murdered Tatiana, and I will use my memories of her to help kill him."

"It's not guaranteed that Leopold will die once this spell is reversed," Grisha reminded them. "He fears death might happen, but it may just be that his power weakens even more."

"I hope he dies. Then I will take Theodora away from this godforsaken place," Thisbe said.

"What about Tyr?" Maggie asked. "You'll be able to see her!"

Thisbe took her spectacles off and began to rub them with her rumpled but clean shirt.

"She can never get back what she has given up in exchange for magic," Grisha whispered.

Thisbe put her glasses back on and said calmly, as if she hadn't heard either of them, "I think seventy-two dragons are still buried. Is that right?"

There had been seventy-seven when the unlucky dragons were first moved to the apartment building. Three had been shot trying to escape, and two had died from a reaction to the spell that was supposed to have put them to sleep.

"Yes," Grisha said.

"You say Tyr thinks it will take about two ounces of water per dragon?" Thisbe asked, not waiting for an answer. "So two times seventy-two is . . . oh, I hate math."

"A little over four liters," Maggie said, glad that her father insisted that math was a vital part of a creative and independent person's education.

"Can you carry that out of the forest?" Thisbe asked Grisha.

"Of course," he said, and, as if to prove it, he spread and flexed his wings.

>—·—<

It was a shorter flight than the one to London, but much bumpier. As soon as Maggie and Grisha landed—in a shallow pond at the edge of a clearing—and were out of the water, Maggie slid off her friend's back, landing with a thump on her bottom. Grisha had scaled to an enormous size the moment he'd caught scent of his old home; each of his paws was now twice as large as when they had taken off.

Maggie stood up and got a good look at his new girth. It was impressive. "How far are we from the rivers?"

"Not far," he said, and led her into the woods until they arrived at a new clearing. "This is where I was captured by Leopold," Grisha said. "I lived with my mother three miles north of here." Being this close to where she had taught him to roar made Grisha sad.

"Did you ever see her again?" Maggie asked.

Grisha was struck by how often she knew his thoughts without walking through his mind the way Thisbe could and did. He shook his head no. "She died about sixty years before Yakov freed me," Grisha said. "Dragons don't live much past five hundred or so."

"How old are you?" Maggie asked.

"Close to two hundred, maybe," he said. "I don't know exactly how old I was when I went into the teapot, but I doubt more than sixty."

"How old is Kator?" Maggie asked.

"About three hundred and seventy, I would guess," Grisha said. "Only Lennox is over five hundred."

"If you get sick before I find a way to see you again, will you ask Kator to keep an eye out for me?" Maggie asked.

"Once you do this, you won't see me again," Grisha said. "And you won't see Kator, either, or any of Vienna's dragons."

"I don't think we know enough about magic to say that," Maggie said.

"I do," Grisha said. After all, if you're born in the forest, you know exactly what magic is. It was odd, he thought, how stories about magic tried to present it as a force for good. Magic was just a force available to those who understood it.

He and Maggie were leaning against two oak trees, looking at how light filtered through the leaves. "Don't agree to give up seeing magic if you're thinking it's temporary," he told her.

"I have to think it's not forever," she said. "It's the only way I'll be able to do it."

"Maggie—"

"Don't," she said. "Let's not talk. Let's just pretend that everything will work out."

Grisha remembered that early on in his enchantment, he had repeatedly told himself that it wasn't forever, that sooner or later the spell would reverse itself and he would be free. As it turned out, he *was* freed, just not in the way he had imagined. So who was he to tell Maggie that things would not work out in some way or another?

"It's getting late," he said. "We'll spend the night by the basin and then fill up the bottles just before we head home."

He dropped onto all fours and she climbed up without hesitating. When he walked there was no turbulence, and the ride was smoother than when flying. Grisha moved slowly, so it was more like sauntering anyway. It was exactly the right way, Maggie thought, to be a part of a forest.

They heard the rivers before they saw them. They emerged from the forest onto a grassy bank. On either side of the bank were two narrow bands of water, which Maggie assumed were the Breg and the Brigach. The small rivers crossed right at the bank's tip and swirled a bit before spilling out into the wide start of the Danube. It was beautiful, but in the normal way of any wide and glorious river.

"Sometimes magic doesn't have to be more than it is," Grisha said, when Maggie complained that none of the three rivers—even where they met—looked particularly special. "People expect that the magical will be extraordinary, but it's often easy to overlook."

He pulled cheese, bread, and a chocolate torte from the basket Alexander had asked the hotel kitchen to pack. He took a long drink of water from the Breg side of the riverbank and filled a cup for Maggie, who looked at it cautiously. "By itself, it's just water," he told her.

The sun had faded away, turning the forest a soft gray. By midnight, it would be black, then dark blue in the very early morning, and then gray again, but this time streaked with pink.

It had been a long day and tomorrow would be another. Grisha made a space between his front paws and Maggie curled up as if she were falling asleep under a table at the Blaue Bar.

She looked up at his long neck and huge chin, thinking of how wonderful it would be when the dragons were freed.

"Try to sleep," Grisha said.

She pretended to sleep, yet struggled to stay awake. She wanted her body to memorize the sound of Grisha's breathing and the forest's smell of spoiled oranges and cinnamon. It was important that she not forget a thing about her time with him—even the feel of damp air upon her skin. If everything went according to plan, memories would be all she had of him.

In the morning, as if by agreement, they neither ate nor spoke, but filled the clay bottles. Maggie put them carefully into a canvas book bag and held it against her chest after taking her seat up on Grisha's back. For now, there was nothing to be done but hold on and close her eyes.

>–•–<

Grisha wasn't sure if he was more worried about the potion working or not working. Either way, the outcome concerned all of Vienna's dragons, so he knew he should tell their leader. Lennox might be old, his scales all white and silver, but he still served as their unofficial yet steady guide.

If Grisha and Maggie's plan worked, all those buried dragons would need help from those who'd stayed above-ground. If the plan didn't work, Grisha would want to try again, but he'd want Vienna's dragons to be involved.

Lennox liked to sleep outside, as all dragons did, but he claimed to be too old to crave a high point. He pre-ferred, he said, to wrap himself around the base of one of the many fountains or sculptures in the elaborate gardens of the Belvedere. He could stay there even during the day and, with his silver-white color, looked part of the marble.

Grisha scaled down to almost human size and sat on one of the benches near the old dragon. He knew that as soon as he told someone what he and Maggie were hoping to do, their private quest would become very real. And he would be that much closer to never seeing her again.

There was a slight movement at the corner of the fountain, and Lennox, in his soft yet mighty voice, said, "Benevolentia Gaudium, are you going to sit there all night or are you going to tell me why you're here?"

Grisha looked into the ancient dragon's gold eyes and realized he was about to do something he'd never done before. In fact, the burning on his face announced that he was already doing it. He was crying.

Lennox unwound himself from the fountain, but did not scale down enough to sit on the bench. Instead he curved around it, making a protective barrier and looking away so that Grisha might have some privacy as his grief burned its way out of his eyes. He could feel little blisters forming on the inside edges of his eyes and along his nose. That fact that his face now hurt made him cry even more.

Ever so delicately, Lennox unfolded a wing and wrapped it around Grisha's shoulders.

"I'm sorry," Grisha said, when the tears finally stopped. "I didn't come here to weep like a baby."

"In point of fact, baby dragons don't weep," Lennox said. "It is generally only done by warriors who have suffered in battle."

"I didn't know that," Grisha said.

"Yes, I imagine a lot of your education was cut short by that teapot."

Now the older dragon scaled down enough to sit on the bench. "Indomitus Ignis says you have been absent from your castle for several days," he said. "Have you received a punishment from the D.E.E?"

"No, that's not it at all," Grisha said. "It's . . . Do you remember the other dragons? The ones whose eyes aren't gold?"

"Best not to think of them," Lennox said. "Their fate has been sealed."

"Maybe not," Grisha said, and told him all that he and Maggie had done and what they hoped would happen the next day. "I came here to ask that if she and I can free them, then will those of us with gold eyes protect and guide them?"

Lennox was very still. Grisha could tell he understood the gravity of the request.

"It would be a remarkable thing to have them back with us," Lennox said. He spoke slowly and with care. "You were right to come. I will see that we take care of them."

"Thank you. I've been worrying over it all. They must be freed, no matter . . ." Grisha trailed off, not sure exactly how to phrase his hesitation.

"But it is a lot to give up," Lennox said. "We have all seen you and the girl child together. It used to be only on the battlefield that such a bond existed between us and a creature from the world of men."

"She would hate to fail," Grisha said. "So I must hope."

"It's a brave thing to do," Lennox said. "It has been unbearable to think of our buried brothers and sisters."

Grisha shook his head against the idea that he was in any way brave.

"Even if you and the girl child—" Lennox said, and Grisha interrupted.

"Maggie," he said. "If Maggie and me."

"Yes, of course. It is very unlikely that you and Maggie can free those tragic beasts. She has no training in magic. And you are both attempting to undo the work of an experienced practitioner."

"The water is the source of the forest's magic," Grisha said. "It will work. It *must.*"

As hard as it would be never to see Maggie again, Grisha knew that failing to free the dragons would be worse.

"And she *is* giving something up," he said. "We know the rules."

"Sometimes those rules work for a novice and sometimes not," Lennox said. "But no matter what happens tomorrow, you have already shown your special purpose."

"*I* haven't done anything," Grisha said. "If our plan works, it will be because of what Maggie does."

"Your father once came to me for advice," Lennox said. "You had taken an extra twenty years to arrive, but your appearance gave no clue of special ability or fate. He was worried and wondered if he should hire a special teacher."

Grisha already knew that his birth had simply been one of magic's odd turns. "They didn't hire anyone," he said.

"I told him to wait and see," Lennox said. "If magic had made you for a special purpose, it would present itself."

Grisha did not feel like talking about his parents. Or the fact that what had presented itself was a sorcerer and a teapot.

"Of all of us, you are the only one who managed to remember," Lennox said. "Of all of us, only you have really looked at this world of men instead of looking back on a world that used to be."

"Every one of us can look at the world," Grisha said. "It's not a special ability."

"Everyone can look at the world," Lennox said. "But only those who pause to see what is wrong can change it."

>—·—<

That night, Grisha didn't go home. Lennox remained in the garden and Grisha found his way to the Belvedere's roof. He could see the Bristol and, just past it, tucked behind the Opera House, the Sacher. He thought of the many times when, as a teapot, he had stood guard in Ella and Rachel's bedroom. Keeping watch didn't mean that the person you loved knew you were there.

"Good night," he whispered, and, quite gently, blew out some smoke.

He watched it float this way and that, until it faded, and disappeared.

# CHAPTER TWENTY-FOUR

# THE EXCHANGE

**THEY HAD ARRANGED TO MEET TYR IN THE SMALL** room at the U4 metro stop. Maggie carried one of the liters of water and an espresso cup. Grisha took charge of the other bottles. To carry them he had to scale down to a small-enough size that he could navigate the maze of hallways without walking on all fours. Under different circumstances, Maggie would have been amused by how short her friend was.

When they arrived at the open, hot space, Maggie hardly noticed the heat. The dragons were all so beautiful. And soon, if all went well, they would be just as beautiful, but free.

"How will they drink if they're asleep?" she asked.

"Our scales have a lot to do with our breath," Grisha told her, "so if you pour the water *on* the dragons, it should work."

"I'd worry less about where to put the water and more about what to do with all of them once they're up," Tyr said.

"They're going to be able to dig their way out, right?" Maggie asked.

"Digging your way out of a place can be very upsetting," Grisha told her, scaling back up to his normal size. "We'll probably lead them out through the tunnels and then to the Stadtpark. They'll adjust to the air and practice scaling. And then we can get dinner at the bar."

"You'll have to feed them in shifts," Maggie said. She tried to imagine so many dragons crammed up against the bar ordering drinks and food. It seemed impossible that she wouldn't get to see it.

"I want you to phrase your intention very carefully," Tyr told her. "When you put the water on them, be very specific about what you want."

"I want the dragons to wake up and be free," Maggie said.

"Yes, of course," Tyr said. "What I meant is that you should describe what you are giving up very carefully."

"Why? What do you mean?"

"I mean exactly what I said," Tyr told her, reminding Maggie of how annoying cats could be.

"Only you know what is precious to you," Grisha explained, "so in order for the water to work, only you can say what is being given away."

"I see," Maggie said, afraid she might not be able to make the water work.

"Just be honest," Grisha said. "Magic can always sense deceit."

Maggie looked at all of the colors spread upon the ground and wondered if the dragons would be sorry not to have a chance to thank her. Or to tell her their stories. She desperately wanted to hear them, but unless she gave up that possibility, no one ever would.

She would not think right now. Nothing good would come of thinking. "Let's start."

"Wait," Grisha said. "Wait. We have to say goodbye."

"No," she said. "I won't do that. You will always be with me, no matter what."

"We're not going to be able to see each other again," he said. "It'll be as if I'm not there."

"It will never be like that," Maggie said. "You will always be there because I *know* you're there."

"You can't take a part of my heart," he told her. "You *are* a part of my heart."

Maggie simply looked at him. There was so much to

say, but not nearly enough time. Grisha leaned forward and put his head gently against hers; first one side and then the other.

"Thank you," Maggie whispered to him. "Thank you."

"You're going to have to help her start," Tyr said, impatient with both of them.

Grisha picked up one of the bottles.

"Promise me you'll make sure they're all safe," Maggie said.

He nodded and poured water into the espresso cup while she looked carefully at the creatures on the floor. Silently at first, and then aloud, she offered up her intention.

"To the world of magic: In return for freeing the dragons, I give you my first and only friend."

She watched the water slip from the cup over the first dragon, who was a marvelous combination of blue, yellow, and green. Slowly, she and Grisha moved among the sleeping dragons, pouring and placing and hoping that her offered exchange was as careful and honest as it needed to be.

For the first twenty or so dragons, nothing changed. Maggie could still see Grisha, and none of the sleeping creatures had woken up. In spite of her very real disappointment, she couldn't help but be relieved. There was no way to imagine a life without Grisha. Because of him, she had traveled without her father and remembered her mother. Plus, she had talked to enchanted cats and one ancient artisan. Along the way, Grisha had somehow helped her to be exactly who she was. She was sorry about the buried dragons, of course, but it was okay that the potion wasn't working. Now she would spend her life as Grisha's friend.

Just as she was turning to tell him this, she saw a movement from the corner of her eye, and a blur of blue and yellowish green.

The room was now completely empty save for a small cat and four clay bottles, one of them hovering in midair. She saw water pour from the bottle into the cup she held. She knew that Grisha's paws held the bottle and what not being able to see those paws meant.

"I guess it's working," Maggie said to Tyr.

The bottle moved from just above her hand to two feet above the ground. Maggie saw how the water she released did not fall straight to the ground, but dispersed as if running over something solid.

"Are they all moving, or only one at a time?" she asked Tyr, holding the cup out for more water.

Tyr was silent.

"Can you describe it to me?" Maggie asked. She felt her throat tighten. There was still no answer, so she took her hands away from the bottle and looked at the cat.

"What's wrong with you? Cat got your tongue?" She laughed, quite pleased with herself, but Tyr remained silent.

Of course. Why hadn't she realized that might happen? In giving away her ability to see dragons, she'd also given up being able to talk to cats, enchanted and otherwise. The world of magic was no longer open to her.

The bottle nudged her and slowly she went back to the task at hand, working until all four bottles were empty and the last one was placed gently on the ground.

>—·—<

When she found herself just outside of the Stadtpark, leaning against a gate and with no idea of how she had gotten there, Maggie wasn't too terribly surprised. Girls who can't talk to cats or see dragons probably can't remain in rooms and tunnels built by those same dragons. Her eyes stung and there was a terrible tightness in her chest.

Someday, she told herself, she would travel to London and look for Yakov Merdinger's great-grandchild. With any luck, Nadia would turn out to be like Ella and able to spot a dragon no matter how old she got. The two of them would sit over a pot of tea every afternoon and eat biscuits. Eventually, Grisha would find them and Maggie would talk to him through Nadia. He would tell her all of his stories and she would tell him hers.

In spite of or maybe even because of this imagined rosy picture, Maggie put her hands over her face and cried until her head hurt. It was the sort of crying that makes it hard to breathe and causes headaches that throb and stab.

Not one person walking by seemed to notice, and for once she was glad that so few people paid attention to things they didn't care about. She wiped her eyes and a feeling of softness settled over her. She was reminded of when she'd seen her mother's paintings in Rome and Grisha had put his paw on her shoulder.

"Grisha?" she asked in a quiet voice. How still would she have to be in order to sense the presence of a creature she could no longer see?

Maggie knew that she might be able to ask Alexander to find Grisha, but for now she needed to keep private what she'd done. Giving up her ability to see or talk with Grisha was the first decision she'd made without asking her father's advice.

The consequences would be hers to face alone.

Slowly, Maggie made her way to the lobby of the Sacher and asked that a pitcher of ice water and two aspirin be sent to her room. Once upstairs, she opened all the windows to let in some fresh air. She stood in front of her pajama drawer for a long time before deciding to leave her stuffed rabbit in peace.

From her window, she could see the tops of the trees lining the Kärntner Ring. The leaves no longer held the rich, deep green of summer, but they had yet to turn the brilliant colors of fall. She watched as the last bit of light left Vienna's sky and a soft, mournful blue-gray blanketed the city's buildings and boulevards.

When Alexander opened her door, asking if she wanted to come down to the bar with him, she shook her head, saying she was too tired.

"What shall I tell Grisha?" he asked.

"Grisha will understand," she said. "Good night."

She imagined Thisbe on the roof of the D.E.E., looking at the very same sky, wishing she could see Tyr. Maybe news of Leopold's death had reached Thisbe and she was already packing up and planning a new life for herself and Theodora.

Or Leopold might still be alive, and Thisbe still at the D.E.E. Maggie hoped that whatever the cat's fate, Thisbe was pleased that what she and Tyr had tried to do forty years ago was now done.

Eventually, when tiredness and hunger finally overcame her, Maggie put herself to bed for the first time since Alexander had hired Grisha. She drew her knees up under her chin and leaned against the pillows on her bed.

Somewhere, because of her, seventy-two dragons were awake and alive in a world not quite willing or ready to accept them. They would settle in bits of forest or empty buildings.

Maggie would never know exactly what became of Vienna's dragons, and because of that she'd always be less herself, but also so much more.

"Good night, Grisha," she said.

After all, even when you can't see it, magic is still there, tucked into shadows and corners. It's visible, but only if you look.

# ACKNOWLEDGMENTS

Holly McGhee helped me to find the story, Taylor Norman created a viable structure, Katie Harnett captured Vienna, and Jennifer Tolo Pierce pulled it all together. Tara Nicole Weyr, Katie Smythe Newman, and Christine Marshall each provided places to write. I am grateful beyond measure. Mary Ciuk reminded me that I knew dragons. For that and much else, thank you.

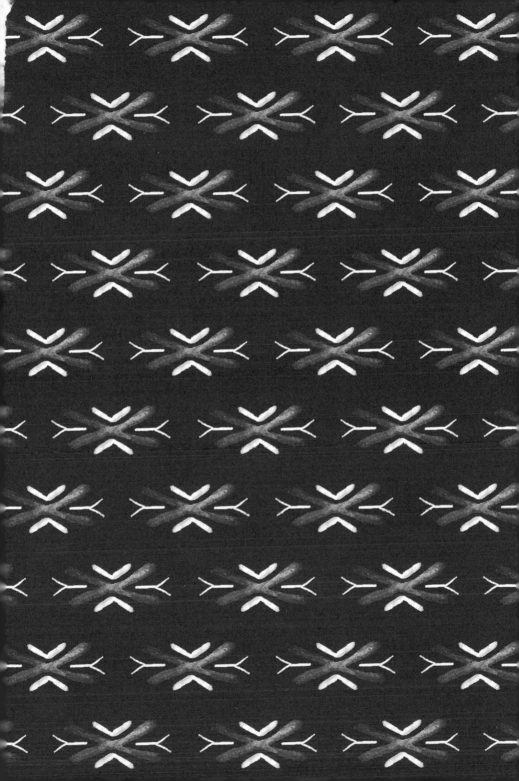